Victorian
SHORT STORIES
Stories of Courtship

W. S. Gilbert

Pharos Books

ISBN: 978-93-59835-83-9
eISBN: 978-93-59839-63-9

©Publisher

Publisher: Pharos Books (P) Ltd.
Plot No.-63, 1st Floor, Main Mother Dairy Road
Pandav Nagar, East Delhi-110092
Phone: 011-40395855, +4049916623
WhatsApp: +91 8368220032
E-mail: sales@pharosbooks.in
Website: www.pharosbooks.in
First Edition: 2024

Victorian Short Stories: Stories of Courtship
W. S. Gilbert

CONTENTS

ANGELA
An Inverted Love Story

By William Schwenk Gilbert

(*The Century Magazine*, September 1890)

I am a poor paralysed fellow who, for many years past, has been confined to a bed or a sofa. For the last six years I have occupied a small room, giving on to one of the side canals of Venice, and having no one about me but a deaf old woman, who makes my bed and attends to my food; and there I eke out a poor income of about thirty pounds a year by making water-colour drawings of flowers and fruit (they are the cheapest models in Venice), and these I send to a friend in London, who sells them to a dealer for small sums. But, on the whole, I am happy and content.

It is necessary that I should describe the position of my room rather minutely. Its only window is about five feet above the water of the canal, and above it the house projects some six feet, and overhangs the water, the projecting portion being supported by stout piles driven into the bed of the canal. This arrangement has the disadvantage (among others) of so limiting my upward view that I am unable to see more than about ten feet of the height of the house immediately opposite to me, although, by reaching as far out of the window as my infirmity will permit, I can see for a considerable distance up and down the canal, which does not exceed fifteen feet in width. But, although I can see but little of the material house opposite, I can see its reflection upside down in the canal, and I take a good deal of inverted interest in such of its inhabitants as show themselves from time to time (always upside down) on its balconies and at its windows.

When I first occupied my room, about six years ago, my attention was directed to the reflection of a little girl of thirteen or so (as nearly as I could judge), who passed every day on a balcony just above the upward range of my limited field of view. She had a glass of flowers and a crucifix on a little table by her side; and as she sat there, in fine weather, from early morning until dark, working assiduously all the time, I concluded that she earned her living by needle-work. She was certainly an industrious little girl, and, as far as I could judge by her upside-down reflection, neat in her dress and pretty. She had an old mother, an invalid, who, on warm days, would sit on the balcony with her, and it interested me to see the little maid wrap the old lady in shawls, and bring pillows for her chair, and a stool for her feet, and every now and again lay down her work and kiss and fondle the old lady for half a minute, and then take up her work again.

Time went by, and as the little maid grew up, her reflection grew down, and at last she was quite a little woman of, I suppose, sixteen or seventeen. I can only work for a couple of hours or so in the brightest part of the day, so I had plenty of time on my hands in which to watch her movements, and sufficient imagination to weave a little romance about her, and to endow her with a beauty which, to a great extent, I had to take for granted. I saw—or fancied that I could see—that she began to take an interest in *my* reflection (which, of course, she could see as I could see hers); and one day, when it appeared to me that she was looking right at it—that is to say when her reflection appeared to be looking right at me—I tried the desperate experiment of nodding to her, and to my intense delight her reflection nodded in reply. And so our two reflections became known to one another.

It did not take me very long to fall in love with her, but a long time passed before I could make up my mind to do more than nod to her every morning, when the old woman moved me from my bed to the sofa at the window, and again in the evening, when the little maid left the balcony for that day. One day, however, when I saw her reflection looking at mine, I nodded to her, and threw a flower into the canal. She nodded several times in return, and I saw her direct her mother's

     Victorian Short Stories: Stories of Courtship

attention to the incident. Then every morning I threw a flower into the water for 'good morning', and another in the evening for 'goodnight', and I soon discovered that I had not altogether thrown them in vain, for one day she threw a flower to join mine, and she laughed and clapped her hands when she saw the two flowers join forces and float away together. And then every morning and every evening she threw her flower when I threw mine, and when the two flowers met she clapped her hands, and so did I; but when they were separated, as they sometimes were, owing to one of them having met an obstruction which did not catch the other, she threw up her hands in a pretty affectation of despair, which I tried to imitate but in an English and unsuccessful fashion. And when they were rudely run down by a passing gondola (which happened not unfrequently) she pretended to cry, and I did the same. Then, in pretty pantomime, she would point downwards to the sky to tell me that it was Destiny that had caused the shipwreck of our flowers, and I, in pantomime, not nearly so pretty, would try to convey to her that Destiny would be kinder next time, and that perhaps tomorrow our flowers would be more fortunate—and so the innocent courtship went on. One day she showed me her crucifix and kissed it, and thereupon I took a little silver crucifix that always stood by me, and kissed that, and so she knew that we were one in religion.

One day the little maid did not appear on her balcony, and for several days I saw nothing of her; and although I threw my flowers as usual, no flower came to keep it company. However, after a time, she reappeared, dressed in black, and crying often, and then I knew that the poor child's mother was dead, and, as far as I knew, she was alone in the world. The flowers came no more for many days, nor did she show any sign of recognition, but kept her eyes on her work, except when she placed her handkerchief to them. And opposite to her was the old lady's chair, and I could see that, from time to time, she would lay down her work and gaze at it, and then a flood of tears would come to her relief. But at last one day she roused herself to nod to me, and then her flower came, day by day, and my flower went forth to join it, and with varying fortunes the two flowers sailed away as of yore.

But the darkest day of all to me was when a good-looking young gondolier, standing right end uppermost in his gondola (for I could see *him* in the flesh), worked his craft alongside the house, and stood talking to her as she sat on the balcony. They seemed to speak as old friends—indeed, as well as I could make out, he held her by the hand during the whole of their interview which lasted quite half an hour. Eventually he pushed off, and left my heart heavy within me. But I soon took heart of grace, for as soon as he was out of sight, the little maid threw two flowers growing on the same stem—an allegory of which I could make nothing, until it broke upon me that she meant to convey to me that he and she were brother and sister, and that I had no cause to be sad. And thereupon I nodded to her cheerily, and she nodded to me, and laughed aloud, and I laughed in return, and all went on again as before.

Then came a dark and dreary time, for it became necessary that I should undergo treatment that confined me absolutely to my bed for many days, and I worried and fretted to think that the little maid and I should see each other no longer, and worse still, that she would think that I had gone away without even hinting to her that I was going. And I lay awake at night wondering how I could let her know the truth, and fifty plans flitted through my brain, all appearing to be feasible enough at night, but absolutely wild and impracticable in the morning. One day—and it was a bright day indeed for me—the old woman who tended me told me that a gondolier had inquired whether the English signor had gone away or had died; and so I learnt that the little maid had been anxious about me, and that she had sent her brother to inquire, and the brother had no doubt taken to her the reason of my protracted absence from the window.

From that day, and ever after during my three weeks of bed-keeping, a flower was found every morning on the ledge of my window, which was within easy reach of anyone in a boat; and when at last a day came when I could be moved, I took my accustomed place on my sofa at the window, and the little maid saw me, and stood on her head (so to speak) and clapped her hands upside down with a delight that was as eloquent as my right-end-up delight could be.

 Victorian Short Stories: Stories of Courtship

And so the first time the gondolier passed my window I beckoned to him, and he pushed alongside, and told me, with many bright smiles, that he was glad indeed to see me well again. Then I thanked him and his sister for their many kind thoughts about me during my retreat, and I then learnt from him that her name was Angela, and that she was the best and purest maiden in all Venice, and that anyone might think himself happy indeed who could call her sister, but that he was happier even than her brother, for he was to be married to her, and indeed they were to be married the next day.

Thereupon my heart seemed to swell to bursting, and the blood rushed through my veins so that I could hear it and nothing else for a while. I managed at last to stammer forth some words of awkward congratulation, and he left me, singing merrily, after asking permission to bring his bride to see me on the morrow as they returned from church.

'For', said he, 'my Angela has known you very long—ever since she was a child, and she has often spoken to me of the poor Englishman who was a good Catholic, and who lay all day long for years and years on a sofa at a window, and she had said over and over again how dearly she wished she could speak to him and comfort him; and one day, when you threw a flower into the canal, she asked me whether she might throw another, and I told her yes, for he would understand that it meant sympathy for one sorely afflicted.'

And so I learned that it was pity, and not love, except indeed such love as is akin to pity, that prompted her to interest herself in my welfare, and there was an end of it all.

For the two flowers that I thought were on one stem were two flowers tied together (but I could not tell that), and they were meant to indicate that she and the gondolier were affianced lovers, and my expressed pleasure at this symbol delighted her, for she took it to mean that I rejoiced in her happiness.

And the next day the gondolier came with a train of other gondoliers, all decked in their holiday garb, and on his gondola sat Angela, happy, and blushing at her happiness. Then he and she entered the house in which I dwelt, and came into my room (and it was strange indeed, after so many years of inversion, to see her with her head above her feet!), and then she wished me happiness and a speedy restoration to good health (which could never be); and I in broken words and with tears in my eyes, gave her the little silver crucifix that had stood by my bed or my table for so many years. And Angela took it reverently, and crossed herself, and kissed it, and so departed with her delighted husband.

And as I heard the song of the gondoliers as they went their way— the song dying away in the distance as the shadows of the sundown closed around me—I felt that they were singing the requiem of the only love that had ever entered my heart.

***

THE PARSON'S DAUGHTER OF OXNEY COLNE

By Anthony Trollope

(*London Review*, 2 March 1861)

The prettiest scenery in all England—and if I am contradicted in that assertion, I will say in all Europe—is in Devonshire, on the southern and southeastern skirts of Dartmoor, where the rivers Dart and Avon and Teign form themselves, and where the broken moor is half cultivated, and the wild-looking uplands fields are half moor. In making this assertion I am often met with much doubt, but it is by persons who do not really know the locality. Men and women talk to me on the matter who have travelled down the line of railway from Exeter to Plymouth, who have spent a fortnight at Torquay, and perhaps made an excursion from Tavistock to the convict prison on Dartmoor. But who knows the glories of Chagford? Who has walked through the parish of Manaton? Who is conversant with Lustleigh Cleeves and Withycombe in the moor? Who has explored Holne Chase? Gentle reader, believe me that you will be rash in contradicting me unless you have done these things.

There or thereabouts—I will not say by the waters of which little river it is washed—is the parish of Oxney Colne. And for those who would wish to see all the beauties of this lovely country a sojourn in Oxney Colne would be most desirable, seeing that the sojourner would then be brought nearer to all that he would delight to visit, than at any other spot in the country. But there is an objection to any such arrangement. There are only two decent houses in the whole parish, and these are—or were when I knew the locality—small and fully occupied by their possessors. The larger and better is the parsonage in which lived the parson and his daughter; and the smaller is the freehold residence of a certain Miss Le Smyrger, who owned a farm of a hundred acres which was rented by one Farmer Cloysey, and who also possessed some thirty acres round her own house which she managed herself, regarding herself to be quite as great in cream as Mr. Cloysey, and altogether superior to him in the article of cider. 'But yeu has to pay no rent, Miss,' Farmer Cloysey would say, when Miss Le Smyrger expressed this opinion of her art in a manner too defiant. 'Yeu pays no rent, or yeu couldn't do it.' Miss Le Smyrger was an old maid, with a pedigree and blood of her own, a hundred and thirty acres of fee-simple land on the borders of Dartmoor, fifty years of age, a constitution of iron, and an opinion of her own on every subject under the sun.

And now for the parson and his daughter. The parson's name was Woolsworthy—or Woolathy as it was pronounced by all those who lived around him—the Rev. Saul Woolsworthy; and his daughter was Patience Woolsworthy, or Miss Patty, as she was known to the Devonshire world of those parts. That name of Patience had not been well chosen for her for she was a hot-tempered damsel, warm in her convictions, and inclined to express them freely. She had but two closely intimate friends in the world, and by both of them this freedom of expression had been fully permitted to her since she was a child. Miss Le Smyrger and her father were well accustomed to her ways, and on the whole well satisfied with them. The former was equally free and equally warm-tempered as herself, and as Mr. Woolsworthy was allowed by his daughter to be quite paramount on his own subject—for he had a subject—he did not object to his daughter being paramount on all others. A pretty girl was Patience Woolsworthy at the time of which I am writing, and one who possessed much that was worthy of remark and admiration had she lived where beauty meets with admiration, or where force of character is remarked. But at Oxney Colne, on the borders of Dartmoor, there were few to appreciate her, and it seemed as though she herself had but little idea of carrying her talent further afield, so that it might not remain for ever wrapped in a blanket.

She was a pretty girl, tall and slender, with dark eyes and black hair. Her eyes were perhaps too round for regular beauty, and her hair was perhaps too crisp; her mouth was large and expressive; her nose was finely formed, though a critic in female form might have declared it to be somewhat broad. But her countenance altogether was very attractive—if only it might be seen without that resolution for dominion which occasionally marred it, though sometimes it even added to her attractions.

It must be confessed on behalf of Patience Woolsworthy that the circumstances of her life had peremptorily called upon her to exercise dominion. She had lost her mother when she was sixteen, and had had neither brother nor sister. She had no neighbours near her fit either from education or rank to interfere in the conduct of her life, excepting always Miss Le Smyrger. Miss Le Smyrger would have done anything for her, including the whole management of her morals and of the parsonage household, had Patience been content with such an arrangement. But much as Patience had ever loved Miss Le Smyrger, she was not content with this, and therefore she had been called on to put forth a strong hand of her own. She had put forth this strong hand early, and hence had come the character which I am attempting to describe. But I must say on behalf of this girl that it was not only over others that she thus exercised dominion. In acquiring that power she had also acquired the much greater power of exercising rule over herself.

But why should her father have been ignored in these family arrangements? Perhaps it may almost suffice to say, that of all living men her father was the man best conversant with the antiquities of the county in which he lived. He was the Jonathan Oldbuck of Devonshire, and especially of Dartmoor,—but without that decision of character which enabled Oldbuck to keep his womenkind in some kind of subjection, and probably enabled him also to see that his weekly bill did not pass their proper limits. Our Mr. Oldbuck, of Oxney Colne, was sadly deficient in these respects. As a parish pastor with but a small cure he did his duty with sufficient energy to keep him, at any rate, from reproach. He was kind and charitable to the poor, punctual in his services, forbearing with the farmers around him, mild with his brother clergymen, and indifferent to aught that bishop or archdeacon might think or say of him. I do not name this latter attribute as a virtue, but as a fact. But all these points were as nothing in the known character of Mr. Woolsworthy, of Oxney Colne. He was the antiquarian of Dartmoor. That was his line of life. It was in that capacity that he was known to the Devonshire world; it was as such that he journeyed about with his humble carpetbag, staying away from his parsonage a night or two at a time; it was in that character that he received now and again stray visitors in the single spare bedroom—not friends asked to see him and his girl because of their friendship—but men who knew something as to this buried stone, or that old land-mark. In all these things his daughter let him have his own way, assisting and encouraging him. That was his line of life, and therefore she respected it. But in all other matters she chose to be paramount at the parsonage.

Mr. Woolsworthy was a little man, who always wore, except on Sundays, grey clothes—clothes of so light a grey that they would hardly have been regarded as clerical in a district less remote. He had now reached a goodly age, being full seventy years old; but still he was wiry and active, and shewed but few symptoms of decay. His head was bald, and the few remaining locks that surrounded it were nearly white. But there was a look of energy about his mouth, and a humour in his light grey eye, which forbade those who knew him to regard him altogether as an old man. As it was, he could walk from Oxney Colne to Priestown, fifteen long Devonshire miles across the moor; and he who could do that could hardly be regarded as too old for work.

But our present story will have more to do with his daughter than with him. A pretty girl, I have said, was Patience Woolsworthy; and one, too, in many ways remarkable. She had taken her outlook into life, weighing the things which she had and those which she had not, in a manner very unusual, and, as a rule, not always desirable for a young lady. The things which she had not were very many. She had not society; she had not a fortune; she had not any assurance of future means of livelihood; she had not high hope of procuring for herself a position in life by marriage; she had not that excitement and pleasure in life which she read of in such books as found their way down to Oxney Colne Parsonage. It would be easy to add to the list of the things which she had not; and this list against herself she made out with the utmost vigour. The things which she had, or those rather which she assured herself of having, were much more easily counted. She had the birth and education of a lady, the strength of a healthy woman, and a will of her own. Such was the list as she made it out for herself, and I protest that I assert no more than the truth in saying that she never added to it either beauty, wit, or talent.

I began these descriptions by saying that Oxney Colne would, of all places, be the best spot from which a tourist could visit those parts of Devonshire, but for the fact that he could obtain there none of the accommodation which tourists require. A brother antiquarian might, perhaps, in those days have done so, seeing that there was, as I have said, a spare bedroom at the parsonage. Any intimate friend of Miss Le Smyrger's might be as fortunate, for she was also so provided at Oxney Colne, by which name her house was known. But Miss Le Smyrger was not given to extensive hospitality, and it was only to those who were bound to her, either by ties of blood or of very old friendship, that she delighted to open her doors. As her old friends were very few in number, as those few lived at a distance, and as her nearest relations were higher in the world than she was, and were said by herself to look down upon her, the visits made to Oxney Colne were few and far between.

But now, at the period of which I am writing, such a visit was about to be made. Miss Le Smyrger had a younger sister who had inherited a property in the parish of Oxney Colne equal to that of the lady who lived there; but this younger sister had inherited beauty also, and she therefore, in early life, had found sundry lovers, one of whom became her husband. She had married a man even then well to do in the world, but now rich and almost mighty; a Member of Parliament, a Lord of this and that board, a man who had a house in Eaton Square, and a park in the north of England; and in this way her course of life had been very much divided from that of our Miss Le Smyrger. But the Lord of the Government board had been blessed with various children, and perhaps it was now thought expedient to look after Aunt Penelope's Devonshire acres. Aunt Penelope was empowered to leave them to whom she pleased; and though it was thought in Eaton Square that she must, as a matter of course, leave them to one of the family, nevertheless a little cousinly intercourse might make the thing more certain. I will not say that this was the sole cause for such a visit, but in these days a visit was to be made by Captain Broughton to his aunt. Now Captain John Broughton was the second son of Alfonso Broughton, of Clapham Park and Eaton Square, Member of Parliament, and Lord of the aforesaid Government Board.

And what do you mean to do with him? Patience Woolsworthy asked of Miss Le Smyrger when that lady walked over from the Colne to say that her nephew John was to arrive on the following morning.

'Do with him? Why, I shall bring him over here to talk to your father.'

'He'll be too fashionable for that, and papa won't trouble his head about him if he finds that he doesn't care for Dartmoor.'

'Then he may fall in love with you, my dear.'

'Well, yes; there's that resource at any rate, and for your sake I dare say I should be more civil to him than papa. But he'll soon get tired of making love to me, and what you'll do then I cannot imagine.'

That Miss Woolsworthy felt no interest in the coming of the Captain I will not pretend to say. The advent of any stranger with whom she would be called on to associate must be matter of interest to her in that secluded place; and she was not so absolutely unlike other young ladies that the arrival of an unmarried young man would be the same to her as the advent of some patriarchal pater-familias. In taking that outlook into life of which I have spoken she had never said to herself that she despised those things from which other girls received the excitement, the joys, and the disappointment of their lives. She had simply given herself to understand that very little of such things would come in her way, and that it behoved her to live—to live happily if such might be possible—without experiencing the need of them. She had heard, when there was no thought of any such visit to Oxney Colne, that John Broughton was a handsome clever man—one who thought much of himself and was thought much of by others—that there had been some talk of his marrying a great heiress, which marriage, however had not taken place through unwillingness on his part, and that he was on the whole a man of more mark in the world than the ordinary captains of ordinary regiments.

Captain Broughton came to Oxney Colne, stayed there a fortnight— the intended period for his projected visit having been fixed at three or four days—and then went his way. He went his way back to his London haunts, the time of the year then being the close of the Easter holy-days; but as he did so he told his aunt that he should assuredly return to her in the autumn.

'And assuredly I shall be happy to see you, John—if you come with a certain purpose. If you have no such purpose, you had better remain away.'

'I shall assuredly come,' the Captain had replied, and then he had gone on his journey.

The summer passed rapidly by, and very little was said between Miss Le Smyrger and Miss Woolsworthy about Captain Broughton. In many respects—nay, I may say, as to all ordinary matters,—no two women could well be more intimate with each other than they were; and more than that, they had the courage each to talk to the other with absolute truth as to things concerning themselves—a courage in which dear friends often fail. But, nevertheless, very little was said between them about Captain John Broughton. All that was said may be here repeated.

'John says that he shall return here in August,' Miss Le Smyrger said as Patience was sitting with her in the parlour at Oxney Colne, on the morning after that gentleman's departure.

'He told me so himself,' said Patience; and as she spoke her round dark eyes assumed a look of more than ordinary self-will. If Miss Le Smyrger had intended to carry the conversation any further she changed her mind as she looked at her companion. Then, as I said, the summer ran by, and towards the close of the warm days of July, Miss Le Smyrger, sitting in the same chair in the same room, again took up the conversation.

'I got a letter from John this morning. He says that he shall be here on the third.'

'Does he?'

'He is very punctual to the time he named.'

'Yes; I fancy that he is a punctual man,' said Patience.

'I hope that you will be glad to see him,' said Miss Le Smyrger.

'Very glad to see him,' said Patience, with a bold clear voice; and then the conversation was again dropped, and nothing further was said till after Captain Broughton's second arrival in the parish.

Four months had then passed since his departure, and during that time Miss Woolsworthy had performed all her usual daily duties in their accustomed course. No one could discover that she had been less careful in her household matters than had been her wont, less willing to go among her poor neighbours, or less assiduous in her attentions to her father. But not the less was there a feeling in the minds of those around her that some great change had come upon her. She would sit during the long summer evenings on a certain spot outside the parsonage orchard, at the top of a small sloping field in which their solitary cow was always pastured, with a book on her knees before her, but rarely reading. There she would sit, with the beautiful view down to the winding river below her, watching the setting sun, and thinking, thinking, thinking—thinking of something of which she had never spoken. Often would Miss Le Smyrger come upon her there, and sometimes would pass her even without a word; but never—never once did she dare to ask of the matter of her thoughts. But she knew the matter well enough. No confession was necessary to inform her that Patience Woolsworthy was in love with John Broughton—ay, in love, to the full and entire loss of her whole heart.

          Victorian Short Stories: Stories of Courtship

On one evening she was so sitting till the July sun had fallen and hidden himself for the night, when her father came upon her as he returned from one of his rambles on the moor. 'Patty,' he said, 'you are always sitting there now. Is it not late? Will you not be cold?'

'No papa,' she said, 'I shall not be cold.'

'But won't you come to the house? I miss you when you come in so late that there's no time to say a word before we go to bed.'

She got up and followed him into the parsonage, and when they were in the sitting-room together, and the door was closed, she came up to him and kissed him. 'Papa,' she said, 'would it make you very unhappy if I were to leave you?'

'Leave me!' he said, startled by the serious and almost solemn tone of her voice. 'Do you mean for always?'

'If I were to marry, papa?'

'Oh, marry! No; that would not make me unhappy. It would make me very happy, Patty, to see you married to a man you would love;—very, very happy; though my days would be desolate without you.'

'That is it, papa. What would you do if I went from you?'

'What would it matter, Patty? I should be free, at any rate, from a load which often presses heavy on me now. What will you do when I shall leave you? A few more years and all will be over with me. But who is it, love? Has anybody said anything to you?'

'It was only an idea, papa. I don't often think of such a thing; but I did think of it then.' And so the subject was allowed to pass by. This had happened before the day of the second arrival had been absolutely fixed and made known to Miss Woolsworthy.

And then that second arrival took place. The reader may have understood from the words with which Miss Le Smyrger authorized her nephew to make his second visit to Oxney Colne that Miss Woolsworthy's passion was not altogether unauthorized. Captain Broughton had been told that he was not to come unless he came with a certain purpose; and having been so told, he still persisted in coming.

There can be no doubt but that he well understood the purport to which his aunt alluded. 'I shall assuredly come,' he had said. And true to his word, he was now there.

Patience knew exactly the hour at which he must arrive at the station at Newton Abbot, and the time also which it would take to travel over those twelve up-hill miles from the station to Oxney. It need hardly be said that she paid no visit to Miss Le Smyrger's house on that afternoon; but she might have known something of Captain Broughton's approach without going thither. His road to the Colne passed by the parsonage-gate, and had Patience sat even at her bedroom window she must have seen him. But on such an evening she would not sit at her bedroom window;—she would do nothing which would force her to accuse herself of a restless longing for her lover's coming. It was for him to seek her. If he chose to do so, he knew the way to the parsonage.

Miss Le Smyrger—good, dear, honest, hearty Miss Le Smyrger, was in a fever of anxiety on behalf of her friend. It was not that she wished her nephew to marry Patience,—or rather that she had entertained any such wish when he first came among them. She was not given to match-making, and moreover thought, or had thought within herself, that they of Oxney Colne could do very well without any admixture from Eaton Square. Her plan of life had been that when old Mr. Woolsworthy was taken away from Dartmoor, Patience should live with her, and that when she also shuffled off her coil, then Patience Woolsworthy should be the maiden-mistress of Oxney Colne—of Oxney Colne and of Mr. Cloysey's farm—to the utter detriment of all the Broughtons. Such had been her plan before nephew John had come among them—a plan not to be spoken of till the coming of that dark day which should make Patience an orphan. But now her nephew had been there, and all was to be altered. Miss Le Smyrger's plan would have provided a companion for her old age; but that had not been her chief object. She had thought more of Patience than of herself, and now it seemed that a prospect of a higher happiness was opening for her friend.

'John,' she said, as soon as the first greetings were over, 'do you remember the last words that I said to you before you went away?' Now, for myself, I much admire Miss Le Smyrger's heartiness, but I do not think much of her discretion. It would have been better, perhaps, had she allowed things to take their course.

'I can't say that I do,' said the Captain. At the same time the Captain did remember very well what those last words had been.

'I am so glad to see you, so delighted to see you, if—if—if—,' and then she paused, for with all her courage she hardly dared to ask her nephew whether he had come there with the express purport of asking Miss Woolsworthy to marry him.

To tell the truth—for there is no room for mystery within the limits of this short story,—to tell, I say, at a word the plain and simple truth, Captain Broughton had already asked that question. On the day before he left Oxney Colne he had in set terms proposed to the parson's daughter, and indeed the words, the hot and frequent words, which previously to that had fallen like sweetest honey into the ears of Patience Woolsworthy, had made it imperative on him to do so. When a man in such a place as that has talked to a girl of love day after day, must not he talk of it to some definite purpose on the day on which he leaves her? Or if he do not, must he not submit to be regarded as false, selfish, and almost fraudulent? Captain Broughton, however, had asked the question honestly and truly. He had done so honestly and truly, but in words, or, perhaps, simply with a tone, that had hardly sufficed to satisfy the proud spirit of the girl he loved. She by that time had confessed to herself that she loved him with all her heart; but she had made no such confession to him. To him she had spoken no word, granted no favour, that any lover might rightfully regard as a token of love returned. She had listened to him as he spoke, and bade him keep such sayings for the drawing-rooms of his fashionable friends. Then he had spoken out and had asked for that hand,—not, perhaps, as a suitor tremulous with hope,—but as a rich man who knows that he can command that which he desires to purchase.

'You should think more of this,' she had said to him at last. 'If you would really have me for your wife, it will not be much to you to return here again when time for thinking of it shall have passed by.' With these words she had dismissed him, and now he had again come back to Oxney Colne. But still she would not place herself at the window to look for him, nor dress herself in other than her simple morning country dress, nor omit one item of her daily work. If he wished to take her at all, he should wish to take her as she really was, in her plain country life, but he should take her also with full observance of all those privileges which maidens are allowed to claim from their lovers. He should curtail no ceremonious observance because she was the daughter of a poor country parson who would come to him without a shilling, whereas he stood high in the world's books. He had asked her to give him all that she had, and that all she was ready to give, without stint. But the gift must be valued before it could be given or received. He also was to give her as much, and she would accept it as being beyond all price. But she would not allow that that which was offered to her was in any degree the more precious because of his outward worldly standing.

She would not pretend to herself that she thought he would come to her that afternoon, and therefore she busied herself in the kitchen and about the house, giving directions to her two maids as though the day would pass as all other days did pass in that household. They usually dined at four, and she rarely, in these summer months, went far from the house before that hour. At four precisely she sat down with her father, and then said that she was going up as far as Helpholme after dinner. Helpholme was a solitary farmhouse in another parish, on the border of the moor, and Mr. Woolsworthy asked her whether he should accompany her.

'Do, papa,' she said, 'if you are not too tired.' And yet she had thought how probable it might be that she should meet John Broughton on her walk. And so it was arranged; but, just as dinner was over, Mr. Woolsworthy remembered himself.

'Gracious me,' he said, 'how my memory is going! Gribbles, from Ivybridge, and old John Poulter, from Bovey, are coming to meet here by appointment. You can't put Helpholme off till tomorrow?'

Patience, however, never put off anything, and therefore at six o'clock, when her father had finished his slender modicum of toddy, she tied on her hat and went on her walk. She started forth with a quick step, and left no word to say by which route she would go. As she passed up along the little lane which led towards Oxney Colne she would not even look to see if he was coming towards her; and when she left the road, passing over a stone stile into a little path which ran first through the upland fields, and then across the moor ground towards Helpholme, she did not look back once, or listen for his coming step.

She paid her visit, remaining upwards of an hour with the old bedridden mother of the farmer of Helpholme. 'God bless you, my darling!' said the old lady as she left her; 'and send you someone to make your own path bright and happy through the world.' These words were still ringing in her ears with all their significance as she saw John Broughton waiting for her at the first stile which she had to pass after leaving the farmer's haggard.

'Patty,' he said, as he took her hand, and held it close within both his own, 'what a chase I have had after you!'

'And who asked you, Captain Broughton?' she answered, smiling. 'If the journey was too much for your poor London strength, could you not have waited till tomorrow morning, when you would have found me at the parsonage?' But she did not draw her hand away from him, or in any way pretend that he had not a right to accost her as a lover.

'No, I could not wait. I am more eager to see those I love than you seem to be.'

'How do you know whom I love, or how eager I might be to see them? There is an old woman there whom I love, and I have thought nothing of this walk with the object of seeing her.' And now, slowly drawing her hand away from him, she pointed to the farmhouse which she had left.

'Patty,' he said, after a minute's pause, during which she had looked full into his face with all the force of her bright eyes; 'I have come from London today, straight down here to Oxney, and from my aunt's house close upon your footsteps after you to ask you that one question. Do you love me?'

'What a Hercules?' she said, again laughing. 'Do you really mean that you left London only this morning? Why, you must have been five hours in a railway carriage and two in a post-chaise, not to talk of the walk afterwards. You ought to take more care of yourself, Captain Broughton!'

He would have been angry with her,—for he did not like to be quizzed,—had she not put her hand on his arm as she spoke, and the softness of her touch had redeemed the offence of her words.

'All that have I done,' said he, 'that I may hear one word from you.'

'That any word of mine should have such potency! But, let us walk on, or my father will take us for some of the standing stones of the moor. How have you found your aunt? If you only knew the cares that have sat on her dear shoulders for the last week past, in order that your high mightyness might have a sufficiency to eat and drink in these desolate half-starved regions.'

'She might have saved herself such anxiety. No one can care less for such things than I do.'

'And yet I think I have heard you boast of the cook of your club.' And then again there was silence for a minute or two.

'Patty,' said he, stopping again in the path; 'answer my question. I have a right to demand an answer. Do you love me?'

'And what if I do? What if I have been so silly as to allow your perfections to be too many for my weak heart? What then, Captain Broughton?'

'It cannot be that you love me, or you would not joke now.'

'Perhaps not, indeed,' she said. It seemed as though she were resolved not to yield an inch in her own humour. And then again they walked on.

'Patty,' he said once more, 'I shall get an answer from you tonight,—this evening; now, during this walk, or I shall return tomorrow, and never revisit this spot again.'

            Victorian Short Stories: Stories of Courtship

'Oh, Captain Broughton, how should we ever manage to live without you?'

'Very well,' he said; 'up to the end of this walk I can bear it all;—and one word spoken then will mend it all.'

During the whole of this time she felt that she was ill-using him. She knew that she loved him with all her heart; that it would nearly kill her to part with him; that she had heard his renewed offer with an ecstasy of joy. She acknowledged to herself that he was giving proof of his devotion as strong as any which a girl could receive from her lover. And yet she could hardly bring herself to say the word he longed to hear. That word once said, and then she knew that she must succumb to her love for ever! That word once said, and there would be nothing for her but to spoil him with her idolatry! That word once said, and she must continue to repeat it into his ears, till perhaps he might be tired of hearing it! And now he had threatened her, and how could she speak it after that? She certainly would not speak it unless he asked her again without such threat. And so they walked on again in silence.

'Patty,' he said at last. 'By the heavens above us you shall answer me. Do you love me?'

She now stood still, and almost trembled as she looked up into his face. She stood opposite to him for a moment, and then placing her two hands on his shoulders, she answered him. 'I do, I do, I do,' she said, 'with all my heart; with all my heart—with all my heart and strength.' And then her head fell upon his breast.

Captain Broughton was almost as much surprised as delighted by the warmth of the acknowledgment made by the eager-hearted passionate girl whom he now held within his arms. She had said it now; the words had been spoken; and there was nothing for her but to swear to him over and over again with her sweetest oaths, that those words were true—true as her soul. And very sweet was the walk down from thence to the parsonage gate. He spoke no more of the distance of the ground, or the length of his day's journey. But he stopped her at every turn that he might press her arm the closer to his own, that he might look into the brightness of her eyes, and prolong his hour of delight. There were no more gibes now on her tongue, no raillery at his London finery, no laughing comments on his coming and going. With downright honesty she told him everything: how she had loved him before her heart was warranted in such a passion; how, with much thinking, she had resolved that it would be unwise to take him at his first word, and had thought it better that he should return to London, and then think over it; how she had almost repented of her courage when she had feared, during those long summer days, that he would forget her; and how her heart had leapt for joy when her old friend had told her that he was coming.

'And yet,' said he, 'you were not glad to see me!'

'Oh, was I not glad? You cannot understand the feelings of a girl who has lived secluded as I have done. Glad is no word for the joy I felt. But it was not seeing you that I cared for so much. It was the knowledge that you were near me once again. I almost wish now that I had not seen you till tomorrow.' But as she spoke she pressed his arm, and this caress gave the lie to her last words.

'No, do not come in tonight,' she said, when she reached the little wicket that led up the parsonage. 'Indeed you shall not. I could not behave myself properly if you did.'

'But I don't want you to behave properly.'

'Oh! I am to keep that for London, am I? But, nevertheless, Captain Broughton, I will not invite you either to tea or to supper tonight.'

'Surely I may shake hands with your father.'

'Not tonight—not till—. John, I may tell him, may I not? I must tell him at once.'

'Certainly,' said he.

'And then you shall see him tomorrow. Let me see—at what hour shall I bid you come?'

'To breakfast.'

'No, indeed. What on earth would your aunt do with her broiled turkey and the cold pie? I have got no cold pie for you.'

'I hate cold pie.'

'What a pity! But, John, I should be forced to leave you directly after breakfast. Come down—come down at two, or three; and then I will go back with you to Aunt Penelope. I must see her tomorrow.' And so at last the matter was settled, and the happy Captain, as he left her, was hardly resisted in his attempt to press her lips to his own.

When she entered the parlour in which her father was sitting, there still were Gribbles and Poulter discussing some knotty point of Devon lore. So Patience took off her hat, and sat herself down, waiting till they should go. For full an hour she had to wait, and then Gribbles and Poulter did go. But it was not in such matters as this that Patience Woolsworthy was impatient. She could wait, and wait, and wait, curbing herself for weeks and months, while the thing waited for was in her eyes good; but she could not curb her hot thoughts or her hot words when things came to be discussed which she did not think to be good.

'Papa,' she said, when Gribbles' long-drawn last word had been spoken at the door. 'Do you remember how I asked you the other day what you would say if I were to leave you?'

'Yes, surely,' he replied, looking up at her in astonishment.

'I am going to leave you now,' she said. 'Dear, dearest father, how am I to go from you?'

'Going to leave me,' said he, thinking of her visit to Helpholme, and thinking of nothing else.

Now there had been a story about Helpholme. That bedridden old lady there had a stalwart son, who was now the owner of the Helpholme pastures. But though owner in fee of all those wild acres and of the cattle which they supported, he was not much above the farmers around him, either in manners or education. He had his merits, however; for he was honest, well to do in the world, and modest withal. How strong love had grown up, springing from neighbourly kindness, between our Patience and his mother, it needs not here to tell; but rising from it had come another love—or an ambition which might have grown to love. The young man, after much thought, had not dared to speak to Miss Woolsworthy, but he had sent a message by Miss Le Smyrger. If there could be any hope for him, he would present himself as a suitor—on trial. He did not owe a shilling in the world, and had money by him—saved. He wouldn't ask the parson for a shilling of fortune. Such had been the tenor of his message, and Miss Le Smyrger had delivered it faithfully. 'He does not mean it,' Patience had said with her stern voice. 'Indeed he does, my dear. You may be sure he is in earnest,' Miss Le Smyrger had replied; 'and there is not an honester man in these parts.'

'Tell him,' said Patience, not attending to the latter portion of her friend's last speech, 'that it cannot be,—make him understand, you know—and tell him also that the matter shall be thought of no more.' The matter had, at any rate, been spoken of no more, but the young farmer still remained a bachelor, and Helpholme still wanted a mistress. But all this came back upon the parson's mind when his daughter told him that she was about to leave him.

'Yes, dearest,' she said; and as she spoke, she now knelt at his knees. 'I have been asked in marriage, and I have given myself away.'

'Well, my love, if you will be happy—'

'I hope I shall; I think I shall. But you, papa?'

'You will not be far from us.'

'Oh, yes; in London.'

'In London.'

'Captain Broughton lives in London generally.'

'And has Captain Broughton asked you to marry him?'

'Yes, papa—who else? Is he not good? Will you not love him? Oh, papa, do not say that I am wrong to love him?'

He never told her his mistake, or explained to her that he had not thought it possible that the high-placed son of the London great man shall have fallen in love with his undowered daughter; but he embraced her, and told her, with all his enthusiasm, that he rejoiced in her joy, and would be happy in her happiness. 'My own Patty,' he said, 'I have ever known that you were too good for this life of ours here.' And then the evening wore away into the night, with many tears but still with much happiness.

Captain Broughton, as he walked back to Oxney Colne, made up his mind that he would say nothing on the matter to his aunt till the next morning. He wanted to think over it all, and to think it over, if possible, by himself. He had taken a step in life, the most important that a man is ever called on to take, and he had to reflect whether or no he had taken it with wisdom.

'Have you seen her?' said Miss Le Smyrger, very anxiously, when he came into the drawing-room.

'Miss Woolsworthy you mean,' said he. 'Yes, I've seen her. As I found her out I took a long walk and happened to meet her. Do you know, aunt, I think I'll go to bed; I was up at five this morning, and have been on the move ever since.'

Miss Le Smyrger perceived that she was to hear nothing that evening, so she handed him his candlestick and allowed him to go to his room.

But Captain Broughton did not immediately retire to bed, nor when he did so was he able to sleep at once. Had this step that he had taken been a wise one? He was not a man who, in worldly matters, had allowed things to arrange themselves for him, as is the case with so many men. He had formed views for himself, and had a theory of life. Money for money's sake he had declared to himself to be bad. Money, as a concomitant to things which were in themselves good, he had declared to himself to be good also. That concomitant in this affair of his marriage, he had now missed. Well; he had made up his mind to that, and would put up with the loss. He had means of living of his own, though means not so extensive as might have been desirable. That it would be well for him to become a married man, looking merely to that state of life as opposed to his present state, he had fully resolved. On that point, therefore, there was nothing to repent. That Patty Woolsworthy was good, affectionate, clever, and beautiful, he was sufficiently satisfied. It would be odd indeed if he were not so satisfied now, seeing that for the last four months he had declared to himself daily that she was so with many inward asseverations. And yet though he repeated now again that he was satisfied, I do not think that he was so fully satisfied of it as he had been throughout the whole of those four months. It is sad to say so, but I fear—I fear that such was the case. When you have your plaything how much of the anticipated pleasure vanishes, especially if it have been won easily!

He had told none of his family what were his intentions in this second visit to Devonshire, and now he had to bethink himself whether they would be satisfied. What would his sister say, she who had married the Honourable Augustus Gumbleton, gold-stick-in-waiting to Her Majesty's Privy Council? Would she receive Patience with open arms, and make much of her about London? And then how far would London suit Patience, or would Patience suit London? There would be much for him to do in teaching her, and it would be well for him to set about the lesson without loss of time. So far he got that night, but when the morning came he went a step further, and began mentally to criticize her manner to himself. It had been very sweet, that warm, that full, that ready declaration of love. Yes; it had been very sweet; but—but—; when, after her little jokes, she did confess her love, had she not been a little too free for feminine excellence? A man likes to be told that he is loved, but he hardly wishes that the girl he is to marry should fling herself at his head!

Ah me! yes; it was thus he argued to himself as on that morning he went through the arrangements of his toilet. 'Then he was a brute,' you say, my pretty reader. I have never said that he was not a brute. But this I remark, that many such brutes are to be met with in the beaten paths of the world's high highway. When Patience Woolsworthy had answered him coldly, bidding him go back to London and think over his love; while it seemed from her manner that at any rate as yet she did not care for him; while he was absent from her, and, therefore, longing for her, the possession of her charms, her talent, and bright honesty of purpose had seemed to him a thing most desirable. Now they were

    Victorian Short Stories: Stories of Courtship

his own. They had, in fact, been his own from the first. The heart of this country-bred girl had fallen at the first word from his mouth. Had she not so confessed to him? She was very nice,—very nice indeed. He loved her dearly. But had he not sold himself too cheaply?

I by no means say that he was not a brute. But whether brute or no he was an honest man, and had no remotest dream, either then, on that morning, or during the following days on which such thoughts pressed more thickly on his mind—of breaking away from his pledged word. At breakfast on that morning he told all to Miss Le Smyrger, and that lady, with warm and gracious intentions, confided to him her purpose regarding her property. 'I have always regarded Patience as my heir,' she said, 'and shall do so still.'

'Oh, indeed,' said Captain Broughton.

'But it is a great, great pleasure to me to think that she will give back the little property to my sister's child. You will have your mother's, and thus it will all come together again.'

'Ah!' said Captain Broughton. He had his own ideas about property, and did not, even under existing circumstances, like to hear that his aunt considered herself at liberty to leave the acres away to one who was by blood quite a stranger to the family.

'Does Patience know of this?' he asked.

'Not a word,' said Miss Le Smyrger. And then nothing more was said upon the subject.

On that afternoon he went down and received the parson's benediction and congratulations with a good grace. Patience said very little on the occasion, and indeed was absent during the greater part of the interview. The two lovers then walked up to Oxney Colne, and there were more benedictions and more congratulations. 'All went merry as a marriage bell', at any rate as far as Patience was concerned. Not a word had yet fallen from that dear mouth, not a look had yet come over that handsome face, which tended in any way to mar her bliss. Her first day of acknowledged love was a day altogether happy, and when she prayed for him as she knelt beside her bed there was no feeling in her mind that any fear need disturb her joy.

I will pass over the next three or four days very quickly, merely saying that Patience did not find them so pleasant as that first day after her engagement. There was something in her lover's manner—something which at first she could not define—which by degrees seemed to grate against her feelings. He was sufficiently affectionate, that being a matter on which she did not require much demonstration; but joined to his affection there seemed to be—; she hardly liked to suggest to herself a harsh word, but could it be possible that he was beginning to think that she was not good enough for him? And then she asked herself the question—was she good enough for him? If there were doubt about that, the match should be broken off, though she tore her own heart out in the struggle. The truth, however, was this,—that he had begun that teaching which he had already found to be so necessary. Now, had any one essayed to teach Patience German or mathematics, with that young lady's free consent, I believe that she would have been found a meek scholar. But it was not probable that she would be meek when she found a self-appointed tutor teaching her manners and conduct without her consent.

So matters went on for four or five days, and on the evening of the fifth day, Captain Broughton and his aunt drank tea at the parsonage. Nothing very especial occurred; but as the parson and Miss Le Smyrger insisted on playing backgammon with devoted perseverance during the whole evening, Broughton had a good opportunity of saying a word or two about those changes in his lady-love which a life in London would require—and some word he said also—some single slight word, as to the higher station in life to which he would exalt his bride. Patience bore it—for her father and Miss Le Smyrger were in the room—she bore it well, speaking no syllable of anger, and enduring, for the moment, the implied scorn of the old parsonage. Then the evening broke up, and Captain Broughton walked back to Oxney Colne with his aunt. 'Patty,' her father said to her before they went to bed, 'he seems to me to be a most excellent young man.' 'Dear papa,' she answered, kissing him. 'And terribly deep in love,' said Mr. Woolsworthy. 'Oh, I don't know about that,' she answered, as she left him with her sweetest smile. But though she could thus smile at her father's joke, she had already made up her mind that there was still something to be learned as to her promised husband before she could place herself altogether in his hands. She would ask him whether he thought himself liable to injury from this proposed marriage; and though he should deny any such thought, she would know from the manner of his denial what his true feelings were.

And he, too, on that night, during his silent walk with Miss Le Smyrger, had entertained some similar thoughts. 'I fear she is obstinate', he had said to himself, and then he had half accused her of being sullen also. 'If that be her temper, what a life of misery I have before me!'

'Have you fixed a day yet?' his aunt asked him as they came near to her house.

'No, not yet; I don't know whether it will suit me to fix it before I leave.'

'Why, it was but the other day you were in such a hurry.'

'Ah—yes-I have thought more about it since then.'

'I should have imagined that this would depend on what Patty thinks,' said Miss Le Smyrger, standing up for the privileges of her sex. 'It is presumed that the gentleman is always ready as soon as the lady will consent.'

'Yes, in ordinary cases it is so; but when a girl is taken out of her own sphere—'

'Her own sphere! Let me caution you, Master John, not to talk to Patty about her own sphere.'

'Aunt Penelope, as Patience is to be my wife and not yours, I must claim permission to speak to her on such subjects as may seem suitable to me.' And then they parted—not in the best humour with each other.

On the following day Captain Broughton and Miss Woolsworthy did not meet till the evening. She had said, before those few ill-omened words had passed her lover's lips, that she would probably be at Miss Le Smyrger's house on the following morning. Those ill-omened words did pass her lover's lips, and then she remained at home. This did not come from sullenness, nor even from anger, but from a conviction that it would be well that she should think much before she met him again. Nor was he anxious to hurry a meeting. His thought—his base thought—was this; that she would be sure to come up to the Colne after him; but she did not come, and therefore in the evening he went down to her, and asked her to walk with him.

They went away by the path that led by Helpholme, and little was said between them till they had walked some mile together. Patience, as she went along the path, remembered almost to the letter the sweet words which had greeted her ears as she came down that way with him on the night of his arrival; but he remembered nothing of that sweetness then. Had he not made an ass of himself during these last six months? That was the thought which very much had possession of his mind.

'Patience,' he said at last, having hitherto spoken only an indifferent word now and again since they had left the parsonage, 'Patience, I hope you realize the importance of the step which you and I are about to take?'

'Of course I do,' she answered: 'what an odd question that is for you to ask!'

'Because,' said he, 'sometimes I almost doubt it. It seems to me as though you thought you could remove yourself from here to your new home with no more trouble than when you go from home up to the Colne.'

'Is that meant for a reproach, John?'

'No, not for a reproach, but for advice. Certainly not for a reproach.'

'I am glad of that.'

'But I should wish to make you think how great is the leap in the world which you are about to take.' Then again they walked on for many steps before she answered him.

'Tell me, then, John,' she said, when she had sufficiently considered what words she would speak;—and as she spoke a dark bright colour suffused her face, and her eyes flashed almost with anger. 'What leap do you mean? Do you mean a leap upwards?'

'Well, yes; I hope it will be so.'

'In one sense, certainly, it would be a leap upwards. To be the wife of the man I loved; to have the privilege of holding his happiness in my hand; to know that I was his own—the companion whom he had chosen out of all the world—that would, indeed, be a leap upward; a leap almost to heaven, if all that were so. But if you mean upwards in any other sense—'

'I was thinking of the social scale.'

'Then, Captain Broughton, your thoughts were doing me dishonour.'

'Doing you dishonour!'

'Yes, doing me dishonour. That your father is, in the world's esteem, a greater man than mine is doubtless true enough. That you, as a man, are richer than I am as a woman is doubtless also true. But you dishonour me, and yourself also, if these things can weigh with you now.'

'Patience,—I think you can hardly know what words you are saying to me.'

'Pardon me, but I think I do. Nothing that you can give me—no gifts of that description—can weigh aught against that which I am giving you. If you had all the wealth and rank of the greatest lord in the land, it would count as nothing in such a scale. If—as I have not doubted—if in return for my heart you have given me yours, then—then—then, you have paid me fully. But when gifts such as those are going, nothing else can count even as a make-weight.'

'I do not quite understand you,' he answered, after a pause. 'I fear you are a little high-flown.' And then, while the evening was still early, they walked back to the parsonage almost without another word.

Captain Broughton at this time had only one more full day to remain at Oxney Colne. On the afternoon following that he was to go as far as Exeter, and thence return to London. Of course it was to be expected, that the wedding day would be fixed before he went, and much had been said about it during the first day or two of his engagement. Then he had pressed for an early time, and Patience, with a girl's usual diffidence, had asked for some little delay. But now nothing was said on the subject; and how was it probable that such a matter could be settled after such a conversation as that which I have related? That evening, Miss Le Smyrger asked whether the day had been fixed. 'No,' said Captain Broughton harshly; 'nothing has been fixed.' 'But it will be arranged before you go.' 'Probably not,' he said; and then the subject was dropped for the time.

'John,' she said, just before she went to bed, 'if there be anything wrong between you and Patience, I conjure you to tell me.'

'You had better ask her,' he replied. 'I can tell you nothing.'

On the following morning he was much surprised by seeing Patience on the gravel path before Miss Le Smyrger's gate immediately after breakfast. He went to the door to open it for her, and she, as she gave him her hand, told him that she came up to speak to him. There was no hesitation in her manner, nor any look of anger in her face. But there was in her gait and form, in her voice and countenance, a fixedness of purpose which he had never seen before, or at any rate had never acknowledged.

'Certainly,' said he. 'Shall I come out with you, or will you come upstairs?'

'We can sit down in the summer-house,' she said; and thither they both went.

'Captain Broughton,' she said—and she began her task the moment that they were both seated—'You and I have engaged ourselves as man and wife, but perhaps we have been over rash.'

'How so?' said he.

'It may be—and indeed I will say more—it is the case that we have made this engagement without knowing enough of each other's character.'

'I have not thought so.'

'The time will perhaps come when you will so think, but for the sake of all that we most value, let it come before it is too late. What would be our fate—how terrible would be our misery, if such a thought should come to either of us after we have linked our lots together.'

There was a solemnity about her as she thus spoke which almost repressed him,—which for a time did prevent him from taking that tone of authority which on such a subject he would choose to adopt. But he recovered himself. 'I hardly think that this comes well from you,' he said.

'From whom else should it come? Who else can fight my battle for me; and, John, who else can fight that same battle on your behalf? I tell you this, that with your mind standing towards me as it does stand at present you could not give me your hand at the altar with true words and a happy conscience. Is it not true? You have half repented of your bargain already. Is it not so?'

He did not answer her; but getting up from his seat walked to the front of the summer-house, and stood there with his back turned upon her. It was not that he meant to be ungracious, but in truth he did not know how to answer her. He had half repented of his bargain.

'John,' she said, getting up and following him so that she could put her hand upon his arm, 'I have been very angry with you.'

'Angry with me!' he said, turning sharp upon her.

'Yes, angry with you. You would have treated me like a child. But that feeling has gone now. I am not angry now. There is my hand;—the hand of a friend. Let the words that have been spoken between us be as though they had not been spoken. Let us both be free.'

'Do you mean it?' he asked.

'Certainly I mean it.' As she spoke these words her eyes were filled with tears in spite of all the efforts she could make to restrain them; but he was not looking at her, and her efforts had sufficed to prevent any sob from being audible.

'With all my heart,' he said; and it was manifest from his tone that he had no thought of her happiness as he spoke. It was true that she had been angry with him—angry, as she had herself declared; but nevertheless, in what she had said and what she had done, she had thought more of his happiness than of her own. Now she was angry once again.

'With all your heart, Captain Broughton! Well, so be it. If with all your heart, then is the necessity so much the greater. You go tomorrow. Shall we say farewell now?'

'Patience, I am not going to be lectured.'

'Certainly not by me. Shall we say farewell now?'

'Yes, if you are determined.'

'I am determined. Farewell, Captain Broughton. You have all my wishes for your happiness.' And she held out her hand to him.

'Patience!' he said. And he looked at her with a dark frown, as though he would strive to frighten her into submission. If so, he might have saved himself any such attempt.

'Farewell, Captain Broughton. Give me your hand, for I cannot stay.' He gave her his hand, hardly knowing why he did so. She lifted it to her lips and kissed it, and then, leaving him, passed from the summer-house down through the wicket-gate, and straight home to the parsonage.

During the whole of that day she said no word to anyone of what had occurred. When she was once more at home she went about her household affairs as she had done on that day of his arrival. When she sat down to dinner with her father he observed nothing to make him think that she was unhappy, nor during the evening was there any expression in her face, or any tone in her voice, which excited his attention. On the following morning Captain Broughton called at the parsonage, and the servant-girl brought word to her mistress that he was in the parlour. But she would not see him. 'Laws miss, you ain't a quarrelled with your beau?' the poor girl said. 'No, not quarrelled,' she said; 'but give him that.' It was a scrap of paper containing a word or two in pencil. 'It is better that we should not meet again. God bless you.' And from that day to this, now more than ten years, they have never met.

   Victorian Short Stories: Stories of Courtship

'Papa,' she said to her father that afternoon, 'dear papa, do not be angry with me. It is all over between me and John Broughton. Dearest, you and I will not be separated.'

It would be useless here to tell how great was the old man's surprise and how true his sorrow. As the tale was told to him no cause was given for anger with anyone. Not a word was spoken against the suitor who had on that day returned to London with a full conviction that now at least he was relieved from his engagement. 'Patty, my darling child,' he said, 'may God grant that it be for the best!'

'It is for the best,' she answered stoutly. 'For this place I am fit; and I much doubt whether I am fit for any other.'

On that day she did not see Miss Le Smyrger, but on the following morning, knowing that Captain Broughton had gone off,—having heard the wheels of the carriage as they passed by the parsonage gate on his way to the station,—she walked up to the Colne.

'He has told you, I suppose?' said she.

'Yes,' said Miss Le Smyrger. 'And I will never see him again unless he asks your pardon on his knees. I have told him so. I would not even give him my hand as he went.'

'But why so, thou kindest one? The fault was mine more than his.'

'I understand. I have eyes in my head,' said the old maid. 'I have watched him for the last four or five days. If you could have kept the truth to yourself and bade him keep off from you, he would have been at your feet now, licking the dust from your shoes.'

'But, dear friend, I do not want a man to lick dust from my shoes.'

'Ah, you are a fool. You do not know the value of your own wealth.'

'True; I have been a fool. I was a fool to think that one coming from such a life as he has led could be happy with such as I am. I know the truth now. I have bought the lesson dearly—but perhaps not too dearly, seeing that it will never be forgotten.'

There was but little more said about the matter between our three friends at Oxney Colne. What, indeed, could be said? Miss Le

Smyrger for a year or two still expected that her nephew would return and claim his bride; but he has never done so, nor has there been any correspondence between them. Patience Woolsworthy had learned her lesson dearly. She had given her whole heart to the man; and, though she so bore herself that no one was aware of the violence of the struggle, nevertheless the struggle within her bosom was very violent. She never told herself that she had done wrong; she never regretted her loss; but yet—yet!—the loss was very hard to bear. He also had loved her, but he was not capable of a love which could much injure his daily peace. Her daily peace was gone for many a day to come.

Her father is still living; but there is a curate now in the parish. In conjunction with him and with Miss Le Smyrger she spends her time in the concerns of the parish. In her own eyes she is a confirmed old maid; and such is my opinion also. The romance of her life was played out in that summer. She never sits now lonely on the hillside thinking how much she might do for one whom she really loved. But with a large heart she loves many, and, with no romance, she works hard to lighten the burdens of those she loves.

As for Captain Broughton, all the world knows that he did marry that great heiress with whom his name was once before connected, and that he is now a useful member of Parliament, working on committees three or four days a week with zeal that is indefatigable. Sometimes, not often, as he thinks of Patience Woolsworthy a smile comes across his face.

***

ANTHONY GARSTIN'S COURTSHIP

By Hubert Crackanthorpe

(Savoy, July 1896)

I

A stampede of huddled sheep, wildly scampering over the slaty shingle, emerged from the leaden mist that muffled the fell-top, and a shrill shepherd's whistle broke the damp stillness of the air. And presently a man's figure appeared, following the sheep down the hillside. He halted a moment to whistle curtly to his two dogs, who, laying back their ears, chased the sheep at top speed beyond the brow; then, his hands deep in his pockets, he strode vigorously forward. A streak of white smoke from a toiling train was creeping silently across the distance: the great, grey, desolate undulations of treeless country showed no other sign of life.

The sheep hurried in single file along a tiny track worn threadbare amid the brown, lumpy grass: and, as the man came round the mountain's shoulder, a narrow valley opened out beneath him—a scanty patchwork of green fields, and, here and there, a whitewashed farm, flanked by a dark cluster of sheltering trees.

The man walked with a loose, swinging gait. His figure was spare and angular: he wore a battered, black felt hat and clumsy, iron-bound boots: his clothes were dingy from long exposure to the weather. He had close-set, insignificant eyes, much wrinkled, and stubbly eyebrows streaked with grey. His mouth was close-shaven, and drawn by his abstraction into hard and taciturn lines; beneath his chin bristled an unkempt fringe of sandy-coloured hair.

When he reached the foot of the fell, the twilight was already blurring the distance. The sheep scurried, with a noisy rustling, across a flat, swampy stretch, over-grown with rushes, while the dogs headed them towards a gap in a low, ragged wall built of loosely-heaped boulders. The man swung the gate to after them, and waited, whistling peremptorily, recalling the dogs. A moment later, the animals reappeared, cringing as they crawled through the bars of the gate. He kicked out at them contemptuously, and mounting a stone stile a few yards further up the road, dropped into a narrow lane.

Presently, as he passed a row of lighted windows, he heard a voice call to him. He stopped, and perceived a crooked, white-bearded figure, wearing clerical clothes, standing in the garden gateway.

'Good-evening, Anthony. A raw evening this.'

'Ay, Mr. Blencarn, it is a bit frittish,' he answered. 'I've jest bin gittin' a few lambs off t'fell. I hope ye're keepin' fairly, an' Miss Rosa too.' He spoke briefly, with a loud, spontaneous cordiality.

'Thank ye, Anthony, thank ye. Rosa's down at the church, playing over the hymns for tomorrow. How's Mrs. Garstin?'

'Nicely, thank ye, Mr. Blencarn. She's wonderful active, is mother.'

'Well, good night to ye, Anthony,' said the old man, clicking the gate.

'Good night, Mr. Blencarn,' he called back.

A few minutes later the twinkling lights of the village came in sight, and from within the sombre form of the square-towered church, looming by the roadside, the slow, solemn strains of the organ floated out on the evening air. Anthony lightened his tread: then paused, listening; but, presently, becoming aware that a man stood, listening also, on the bridge some few yards distant, he moved forward again. Slackening his pace, as he approached, he eyed the figure keenly; but the man paid no heed to him, remaining, with his back turned, gazing over the parapet into the dark, gurgling stream.

Anthony trudged along the empty village street, past the gleaming squares of ruddy gold, starting on either side out of the darkness. Now and then he looked furtively backwards. The straight open road lay behind him, glimmering wanly: the organ seemed to have ceased: the figure on the bridge had left the parapet, and appeared to be moving away towards the church. Anthony halted, watching it till it had disappeared into the blackness beneath the churchyard trees. Then, after a moment's hesitation, he left the road, and mounted an upland meadow towards his mother's farm.

It was a bare, oblong house. In front, a whitewashed porch, and a narrow garden-plot, enclosed by a low iron railing, were dimly discernible: behind, the steep fell-side loomed like a monstrous, mysterious curtain hung across the night. He passed round the back into the twilight of a wide yard, cobbled and partially grass-grown, vaguely flanked by the shadowy outlines of long, low farm-buildings. All was wrapped in darkness: somewhere overhead a bat fluttered, darting its puny scream.

Inside, a blazing peat-fire scattered capering shadows across the smooth, stone floor, flickered among the dim rows of hams suspended from the ceiling and on the panelled cupboards of dark, glistening oak. A servant-girl, spreading the cloth for supper, clattered her clogs in and out of the kitchen: old Mrs. Garstin was stooping before the hearth, tremulously turning some girdle-cakes that lay roasting in the embers.

At the sound of Anthony's heavy tread in the passage, she rose, glancing sharply at the clock above the chimney-piece. She was a heavy-built woman, upright, stalwart almost, despite her years. Her face was gaunt and sallow; deep wrinkles accentuated the hardness of her features. She wore a black widow's cap above her iron-grey hair, gold-rimmed spectacles, and a soiled, chequered apron.

'Ye're varra late, Tony,' she remarked querulously.

He unloosened his woollen neckerchief, and when he had hung it methodically with his hat behind the door, answered:

"Twas terrible thick on t' fell-top, an' them two bitches be that senseless.'

She caught his sleeve, and, through her spectacles, suspiciously scrutinized his face.

'Ye did na meet wi' Rosa Blencarn?'

'Nay, she was in church, hymn-playin', wi' Luke Stock hangin' roond door,' he retorted bitterly, rebuffing her with rough impatience.

She moved away, nodding sententiously to herself. They began supper: neither spoke: Anthony sat slowly stirring his tea, and staring moodily into the flames: the bacon on his plate lay untouched. From time to time his mother, laying down her knife and fork, looked across at him in unconcealed asperity, pursing her wide, ungainly mouth. At last, abruptly setting down her cup, she broke out:

'I wonder ye hav'na mare pride, Tony. For hoo lang are ye goin' t' continue settin' mopin' and broodin' like a seck sheep? Ye'll jest mak yesself ill, an' then I reckon what ye'll prove satisfied. Ay, but I wonder ye hav'na more pride.'

But he made no answer, remaining unmoved, as if he had not heard.

Presently, half to himself, without raising his eyes, he murmured:

'Luke be goin' South, Monday.'

'Well, ye canna tak' oop wi' his leavin's anyways. It hasna coom't that, has it? Ye doan't intend settin' all t' parish a laughin' at ye a second occasion?'

He flushed dully, and bending over his plate, mechanically began his supper.

'Wa dang it,' he broke out a minute later, 'd'ye think I heed the cacklin' o' fifty parishes? Na, not I,' and, with a short, grim laugh, he brought his fist down heavily on the oak table.

'Ye're daft, Tony,' the old woman blurted.

'Daft or na daft, I tell ye this, mother, that I be forty-six year o' age this back-end, and there be some things I will na listen to. Rosa Blencarn's bonny enough for me.'

'Ay, bonny enough—I've na patience wi' ye. Bonny enough— tricked oot in her furbelows, gallivantin' wi' every royster fra Pe'rith. Bonny enough—that be all ye think on. She's bin a proper parson's niece—the giddy, feckless creature, an she'd mak' ye a proper sort o' wife, Tony Garstin, ye great, fond booby.'

She pushed back her chair, and, hurriedly clattering the crockery, began to clear away the supper.

'T' hoose be mine, t' Lord be praised,' she continued in a loud, hard voice, 'an' as long as he spare me, Tony, I'll na see Rosa Blencarn set foot inside it.'

Anthony scowled, without replying, and drew his chair to the hearth. His mother bustled about the room behind him. After a while she asked:

'Did ye pen t' lambs in t' back field?'

'Na, they're in Hullam bottom,' he answered curtly.

The door closed behind her, and by and by he could hear her moving overhead. Meditatively blinking, he filled his pipe clumsily, and pulling a crumpled newspaper from his pocket, sat on over the smouldering fire, reading and stolidly puffing.

II

The music rolled through the dark, empty church. The last, leaden flicker of daylight glimmered in through the pointed windows, and beyond the level rows of dusky pews, tenanted only by a litter of prayer-books, two guttering candles revealed the organ pipes, and the young girl's swaying figure.

She played vigorously. Once or twice the tune stumbled, and she recovered it impatiently, bending over the key-board, showily flourishing her wrists as she touched the stops. She was bare-headed (her hat and cloak lay beside her on a stool). She had fair, fluffy hair, cut short behind her neck; large, round eyes, heightened by a fringe of dark lashes; rough, ruddy cheeks, and a rosy, full-lipped, unstable mouth. She was dressed quite simply, in a black, close-fitting bodice, a little frayed at the sleeves. Her hands and neck were coarsely fashioned: her comeliness was brawny, literal, unfinished, as it were.

When at last the ponderous chords of the Amen faded slowly into the twilight, flushed, breathing a little quickly, she paused, listening to the stillness of the church. Presently a small boy emerged from behind the organ.

'Good evenin', Miss Rosa', he called, trotting briskly away down the aisle.

'Good night, Robert', she answered, absently.

After a while, with an impatient gesture, as if to shake some importunate thought from her mind, she rose abruptly, pinned on her hat, threw her cloak round her shoulders, blew out the candles, and groped her way through the church, towards the half-open door. As she hurried along the narrow pathway that led across the churchyard, of a sudden, a figure started out of the blackness.

'Who's that?' she cried, in a loud, frightened voice.

A man's uneasy laugh answered her.

'It's only me, Rosa. I didna' think t' scare ye. I've bin waitin' for ye, this hoor past.'

She made no reply, but quickened her pace. He strode on beside her.

'I'm off, Monday, ye know,' he continued. And, as she said nothing, 'Will ye na stop jest a minnit? I'd like t' speak a few words wi' ye before I go, an tomorrow I hev t' git over t' Scarsdale betimes,' he persisted.

'I don't want t' speak wi' ye: I don't want ever to see ye agin. I jest hate the sight o' ye.' She spoke with a vehement, concentrated hoarseness.

'Nay, but ye must listen to me. I will na be put off wi' fratchin speeches.'

And gripping her arm, he forced her to stop.

'Loose me, ye great beast,' she broke out.

'I'll na hould ye, if ye'll jest stand quiet-like. I meant t' speak fair t' ye, Rosa.'

They stood at a bend in the road, face to face quite close together. Behind his burly form stretched the dimness of a grey, ghostly field.

'What is't ye hev to say to me? Hev done wi' it quick,' she said sullenly.

'It be jest this, Rosa,' he began with dogged gravity. 'I want t' tell ye that ef any trouble comes t'ye after I'm gone—ye know t' what I refer—I want t' tell ye that I'm prepared t' act square by ye. I've written out on an envelope my address in London. Luke Stock, care o' Purcell and Co., Smithfield Market, London.'

'Ye're a bad, sinful man. I jest hate t' sight o' ye. I wish ye were dead.'

'Ay, but I reckon what ye'd ha best thought o' that before. Ye've changed yer whistle considerably since Tuesday. Nay, hould on,' he added, as she struggled to push past him. 'Here's t' envelope.'

She snatched the paper, and tore it passionately, scattering the fragments on to the road. When she had finished, he burst out angrily:

'Ye cussed, unreasonable fool.'

'Let me pass, ef ye've nought mare t'say,' she cried.

'Nay, I'll na part wi' ye this fashion. Ye can speak soft enough when ye choose.' And seizing her shoulders, he forced her backwards against the wall.

'Ye do look fine, an' na mistake, when ye're jest ablaze wi' ragin',' he laughed bluntly, lowering his face to hers.

'Loose me, loose me, ye great coward,' she gasped, striving to free her arms.

Holding her fast, he expostulated:

'Coom, Rosa, can we na part friends?'

'Part friends, indeed,' she retorted bitterly. 'Friends wi' the likes o' you. What d'ye tak me for? Let me git home, I tell ye. An' please God I'll never set eyes on ye again. I hate t' sight o' ye.'

'Be off wi' ye, then,' he answered, pushing her roughly back into the road. 'Be off wi' ye, ye silly. Ye canna say I hav na spak fair t' ye, an', by goom, ye'll na see me shally-wallyin this fashion agin. Be off wi' ye: ye can jest shift for yerself, since ye canna keep a civil tongue in yer head.'

The girl, catching at her breath, stood as if dazed, watching his retreating figure; then starting forward at a run, disappeared up the hill, into the darkness.

III

Old Mr. Blencarn concluded his husky sermon. The scanty congregation, who had been sitting, stolidly immobile in their stiff, Sunday clothes, shuffled to their feet, and the pewful of school children, in clamorous chorus, intoned the final hymn. Anthony stood near the organ, absently contemplating, while the rude melody resounded through the church, Rosa's deft manipulation of the key-board. The rugged lines of his face were relaxed to a vacant, thoughtful limpness, that aged his expression not a little: now and then, as if for reference, he glanced questioningly at the girl's profile.

A few minutes later the service was over, and the congregation sauntered out down the aisle. A gawky group of men remained loitering by the church door: one of them called to Anthony; but, nodding curtly, he passed on, and strode away down the road, across the grey upland meadows, towards home. As soon as he had breasted the hill, however, and was no longer visible from below, he turned abruptly to the left, along a small, swampy hollow, till he had reached the lane that led down from the fell-side.

He clambered over a rugged, moss-grown wall, and stood, gazing expectantly down the dark, disused roadway; then, after a moment's hesitation, perceiving nobody, seated himself beneath the wall, on a projecting slab of stone.

Overhead hung a sombre, drifting sky. A gusty wind rollicked down from the fell—huge masses of chilly grey, stripped of the last night's mist. A few dead leaves fluttered over the stones, and from off the fell-side there floated the plaintive, quavering rumour of many bleating sheep.

Before long, he caught sight of two figures coming towards him, slowly climbing the hill. He sat awaiting their approach, fidgeting with his sandy beard, and abstractedly grinding the ground beneath his heel. At the brow they halted: plunging his hands deep into his pockets, he strolled sheepishly towards them.

'Ah! good day t' ye, Anthony,' called the old man, in a shrill, breathless voice. "Tis a long hill, an' my legs are not what they were.

Time was when I'd think nought o' a whole day's tramp on t' fells. Ay, I'm gittin' feeble, Anthony, that's what 'tis. And if Rosa here wasn't the great, strong lass she is, I don't know how her old uncle'd manage;' and he turned to the girl with a proud, tremulous smile.

'Will ye tak my arm a bit, Mr. Blencarn? Miss Rosa'll be tired, likely,' Anthony asked.

'Nay, Mr. Garstin, but I can manage nicely,' the girl interrupted sharply.

Anthony looked up at her as she spoke. She wore a straw hat, trimmed with crimson velvet, and a black, fur-edged cape, that seemed to set off mightily the fine whiteness of her neck. Her large, dark eyes were fixed upon him. He shifted his feet uneasily, and dropped his glance.

She linked her uncle's arm in hers, and the three moved slowly forward. Old Mr. Blencarn walked with difficulty, pausing at intervals for breath. Anthony, his eyes bent on the ground, sauntered beside him, clumsily kicking at the cobbles that lay in his path.

When they reached the vicarage gate, the old man asked him to come inside.

'Not jest now, thank ye, Mr. Blencarn. I've that lot o' lambs t' see to before dinner. It's a grand marnin', this,' he added, inconsequently.

'Uncle's bought a nice lot o' Leghorns, Tuesday,' Rosa remarked. Anthony met her gaze; there was a grave, subdued expression on her face this morning, that made her look more of a woman, less of a girl.

'Ay, do ye show him the birds, Rosa. I'd be glad to have his opinion on 'em.'

The old man turned to hobble into the house, and Rosa, as she supported his arm, called back over her shoulder:

'I'll not be a minute, Mr. Garstin.'

Anthony strolled round to the yard behind the house, and waited, watching a flock of glossy-white poultry that strutted, perkily pecking, over the grass-grown cobbles.

'Ay, Miss Rosa, they're a bonny lot,' he remarked, as the girl joined him.

'Are they not?' she rejoined, scattering a handful of corn before her.

The birds scuttled across the yard with greedy, outstretched necks. The two stood, side by side, gazing at them.

'What did he give for 'em?' Anthony asked.

'Fifty-five shillings.'

'Ay,' he assented, nodding absently.

'Was Dr. Sanderson na seein' o' yer father yesterday?' he asked, after a moment.

'He came in t' forenoon. He said he was jest na worse.'

'Ye knaw, Miss Rosa, as I'm still thinkin' on ye,' he began abruptly, without looking up.

'I reckon it ain't much use,' she answered shortly, scattering another handful of corn towards the birds. 'I reckon I'll never marry. I'm jest weary o' bein' courted—'

'I would na weary ye wi' courtin',' he interrupted.

She laughed noisily.

'Ye are a queer customer, an' na mistake.'

'I'm a match for Luke Stock anyway,' he continued fiercely. 'Ye think nought o' taking oop wi' him—about as ranty, wild a young feller as ever stepped.'

The girl reddened, and bit her lip.

'I don't know what you mean, Mr. Garstin. It seems to me ye're might hasty in jumpin' t' conclusions.'

'Mabbe I kin see a thing or two,' he retorted doggedly.

'Luke Stock's gone to London, anyway.'

'Ay, an' a powerful good job too, in t' opinion o' some folks.'

'Ye're jest jealous,' she exclaimed, with a forced titter. 'Ye're jest jealous o' Luke Stock.'

'Nay, but ye need na fill yer head wi' that nonsense. I'm too deep set on ye t' feel jealousy,' he answered, gravely.

The smile faded from her face, as she murmured:

'I canna mak ye out, Mr. Garstin.'

'Nay, that ye canna. An' I suppose it's natural, considerin' ye're little more than a child, an' I'm a'most old enough to be yer father,' he retorted, with blunt bitterness.

'But ye know yer mother's took that dislike t' me. She'd never abide the sight o' me at Hootsey.'

He remained silent a moment, moodily reflecting.

'She'd jest ha't' git ower it. I see nought in that objection,' he declared.

'Nay, Mr. Garstin, it canna be. Indeed it canna be at all. Ye'd best jest put it right from yer mind, once and for all.'

'I'd jest best put it off my mind, had I? Ye talk like a child!' he burst out scornfully. 'I intend ye t' coom t' love me, an' I will na tak ye till ye do. I'll jest go on waitin' for ye, an', mark my words, my day 'ull coom at last.'

He spoke loudly, in a slow, stubborn voice, and stepped suddenly towards her. With a faint, frightened cry she shrank back into the doorway of the hen-house.

'Ye talk like a prophet. Ye sort o' skeer me.'

He laughed grimly, and paused, reflectively scanning her face. He seemed about to continue in the same strain; but, instead, turned abruptly on his heel, and strode away through the garden gate.

IV

For three hundred years there had been a Garstin at Hootsey: generation after generation had tramped the grey stretch of upland, in the spring-time scattering their flocks over the fell-sides, and, at the 'back-end', on dark, winter afternoons, driving them home again, down the broad bridle-path that led over the 'raise'. They had been a race of few words, 'keeping themselves to themselves', as the phrase goes; beholden to no man, filled with a dogged, churlish pride—an upright, old-fashioned race, stubborn, long-lived, rude in speech, slow of resolve.

Anthony had never seen his father, who had died one night, upon the fell-top, he and his shepherd, engulfed in the great snowstorm of 1849. Folks had said that he was the only Garstin who had failed to make old man's bones.

After his death, Jake Atkinson, from Ribblehead in Yorkshire, had come to live at Hootsey. Jake was a fine farmer, a canny bargainer, and very handy among the sheep, till he took to drink, and roystering every week with the town wenches up at Carlisle. He was a corpulent, deep-voiced, free-handed fellow: when his time came, though he died very hardly, he remained festive and convivial to the last. And for years afterwards, in the valley, his memory lingered: men spoke of him regretfully, recalling his quips, his feats of strength, and his choice breed of Herdwicke rams. But he left behind him a host of debts up at Carlisle, in Penrith, and in almost every market town—debts that he had long ago pretended to have paid with money that belonged to his sister. The widow Garstin sold the twelve Herdwicke rams, and nine acres of land: within six weeks she had cleared off every penny, and for thirteen months, on Sundays, wore her mourning with a mute, forbidding grimness: the bitter thought that, unbeknown to her, Jake had acted dishonestly in money matters, and that he had ended his days in riotous sin, soured her pride, imbued her with a rancorous hostility against all the world. For she was a very proud woman, independent, holding her head high, so folks said, like a Garstin bred and born; and Anthony, although some reckoned him quiet and of little account, came to take after her as he grew into manhood.

She took into her own hands the management of the Hootsey farm, and set the boy to work for her along with the two farm servants. It was twenty-five years now since his uncle Jake's death: there were grey hairs in his sandy beard; but he still worked for his mother, as he had done when a growing lad.

Victorian Short Stories: Stories of Courtship

And now that times were grown to be bad (of late years the price of stock had been steadily falling; and the hay harvests had drifted from bad to worse) the widow Garstin no longer kept any labouring men; but lived, she and her son, year in and year out, in a close parsimonious way.

That had been Anthony Garstin's life—a dull, eventless sort of business, the sluggish incrustation of monotonous years. And until Rosa Blencarn had come to keep house for her uncle, he had never thought twice on a woman's face.

The Garstins had always been good church-goers, and Anthony, for years, had acted as churchwarden. It was one summer evening, up at the vicarage, whilst he was checking the offertory account, that he first set eyes upon her. She was fresh back from school at Leeds: she was dressed in a white dress: she looked, he thought, like a London lady.

She stood by the window, tall and straight and queenly, dreamily gazing out into the summer twilight, whilst he and her uncle sat over their business. When he rose to go, she glanced at him with quick curiosity; he hurried away, muttering a sheepish good night.

The next time that he saw her was in church on Sunday. He watched her shyly, with a hesitating, reverential discretion: her beauty seemed to him wonderful, distant, enigmatic. In the afternoon, young Mrs. Forsyth, from Longscale, dropped in for a cup of tea with his mother, and the two set off gossiping of Rosa Blencarn, speaking of her freely, in tones of acrimonious contempt. For a long while he sat silent, puffing at his pipe; but at last, when his mother concluded with, 'She looks t' me fair stuck-oop, full o' toonish airs an' graces,' despite himself, he burst out: 'Ye're jest wastin' yer breath wi' that cackle. I reckon Miss Blencarn's o' a different clay to us folks.' Young Mrs. Forsyth tittered immoderately, and the next week it was rumoured about the valley that 'Tony Garstin was gone luny over t' parson's niece.'

But of all this he knew nothing—keeping to himself, as was his wont, and being, besides, very busy with the hay harvest—until one day, at dinner-time, Henry Sisson asked if he'd started his courting;

Jacob Sowerby cried that Tony'd been too slow in getting to work, for that the girl had been seen spooning in Crosby Shaws with Curbison the auctioneer, and the others (there were half-a-dozen of them lounging round the hay-waggon) burst into a boisterous guffaw. Anthony flushed dully, looking hesitatingly from the one to the other; then slowly put down his beer-can, and of a sudden, seizing Jacob by the neck, swung him heavily on the grass. He fell against the waggon-wheel, and when he rose the blood was streaming from an ugly cut in his forehead. And henceforward Tony Garstin's courtship was the common jest of all the parish.

As yet, however, he had scarcely spoken to her, though twice he had passed her in the lane that led up to the vicarage. She had given him a frank, friendly smile; but he had not found the resolution to do more than lift his hat. He and Henry Sisson stacked the hay in the yard behind the house; there was no further mention made of Rosa Blencarn; but all day long Anthony, as he knelt thatching the rick, brooded over the strange sweetness of her face, and on the fell-top, while he tramped after the ewes over the dry, crackling heather, and as he jogged along the narrow, rickety road, driving his cartload of lambs into the auction mart.

Thus, as the weeks slipped by, he was content with blunt, wistful ruminations upon her indistinct image. Jacob Sowerby's accusation, and several kindred innuendoes let fall by his mother, left him coolly incredulous; the girl still seemed to him altogether distant; but from the first sight of her face he had evolved a stolid, unfaltering conception of her difference from the ruck of her sex.

But one evening, as he passed the vicarage on his way down from the fells, she called to him, and with a childish, confiding familiarity asked for advice concerning the feeding of the poultry. In his eagerness to answer her as best he could, he forgot his customary embarrassment, and grew, for the moment, almost voluble, and quite at his ease in her presence. Directly her flow of questions ceased, however, the returning perception of her rosy, hesitating smile, and of her large, deep eyes looking straight into his face, perturbed him strangely, and, reddening, he remembered the quarrel in the hay-field and the tale of Crosby Shaws.

After this, the poultry became a link between them—a link which he regarded in all seriousness, blindly unconscious that there was aught else to bring them together, only feeling himself in awe of her, because of her schooling, her townish manners, her ladylike mode of dress. And soon, he came to take a sturdy, secret pride in her friendly familiarity towards him. Several times a week he would meet her in the lane, and they would loiter a moment together; she would admire his dogs, though he assured her earnestly that they were but sorry curs; and once, laughing at his staidness, she nick-named him 'Mr. Churchwarden'.

That the girl was not liked in the valley he suspected, curtly attributing her unpopularity to the women's senseless jealousy. Of gossip concerning her he heard no further hint; but instinctively, and partly from that rugged, natural reserve of his, shrank from mentioning her name, even incidentally, to his mother.

Now, on Sunday evenings, he often strolled up to the vicarage, each time quitting his mother with the same awkward affectation of casualness; and, on his return, becoming vaguely conscious of how she refrained from any comment on his absence, and appeared oddly oblivious of the existence of parson Blencarn's niece.

She had always been a sour-tongued woman; but, as the days shortened with the approach of the long winter months, she seemed to him to grow more fretful than ever; at times it was almost as if she bore him some smouldering, sullen resentment. He was of stubborn fibre, however, toughened by long habit of a bleak, unruly climate; he revolved the matter in his mind deliberately, and when, at last, after much plodding thought, it dawned upon him that she resented his acquaintance with Rosa Blencarn, he accepted the solution with an unflinching phlegm, and merely shifted his attitude towards the girl, calculating each day the likelihood of his meeting her, and making, in her presence, persistent efforts to break down, once for all, the barrier of his own timidity. He was a man not to be clumsily driven, still less, so he prided himself, a man to be craftily led.

It was close upon Christmas time before the crisis came. His mother was just home from Penrith market. The spring-cart stood in the yard, the old grey horse was steaming heavily in the still, frosty air.

'I reckon ye've come fast. T' ould horse is over hot,' he remarked bluntly, as he went to the animal's head.

She clambered down hastily, and, coming to his side, began breathlessly:

'Ye ought t' hev coom t' market, Tony. There's bin pretty goin's on in Pe'rith today. I was helpin' Anna Forsyth t' choose six yards o' sheetin' in Dockroy, when we sees Rosa Blencarn coom oot o' t' 'Bell and Bullock' in company we' Curbison and young Joe Smethwick. Smethwick was fair reelin' drunk, and Curbison and t' girl were a-houldin' on to him, to keep him fra fallin'; and then, after a bit, he puts his arm round the girl t' stiddy hisself, and that fashion they goes off, right oop t' public street—'

He continued to unload the packages, and to carry them mechanically one by one into the house. Each time, when he reappeared, she was standing by the steaming horse, busy with her tale.

'An' on t' road hame we passed t' three on' em in Curbison's trap, with Smethwick leein' in t' bottom, singin' maudlin' songs. They were passin' Dunscale village, an't' folks coom runnin' oot o' houses t' see 'em go past—'

He led the cart away towards the stable, leaving her to cry the remainder after him across the yard.

Half-an-hour later he came in for his dinner. During the meal not a word passed between them, and directly he had finished he strode out of the house. About nine o'clock he returned, lit his pipe, and sat down to smoke it over the kitchen fire.

'Where've ye bin, Tony?' she asked.

'Oop t' vicarage, courtin',' he retorted defiantly, with his pipe in his mouth.

This was ten months ago; ever since he had been doggedly waiting. That evening he had set his mind on the girl, he intended to have her;

and while his mother gibed, as she did now upon every opportunity, his patience remained grimly unflagging. She would remind him that the farm belonged to her, that he would have to wait till her death before he could bring the hussy to Hootsey: he would retort that as soon as the girl would have him, he intended taking a small holding over at Scarsdale. Then she would give way, and for a while piteously upbraid him with her old age, and with the memory of all the years she and he had spent together, and he would comfort her with a display of brusque, evasive remorse.

But, none the less, on the morrow, his thoughts would return to dwell on the haunting vision of the girl's face, while his own rude, credulous chivalry, kindled by the recollection of her beauty, stifled his misgivings concerning her conduct.

Meanwhile she dallied with him, and amused herself with the younger men. Her old uncle fell ill in the spring, and could scarcely leave the house. She declared that she found life in the valley intolerably dull, that she hated the quiet of the place, that she longed for Leeds, and the exciting bustle of the streets; and in the evenings she wrote long letters to the girl-friends she had left behind there, describing with petulant vivacity her tribe of rustic admirers. At the harvest-time she went back on a fortnight's visit to friends; the evening before her departure she promised Anthony to give him her answer on her return. But, instead, she avoided him, pretended to have promised in jest, and took up with Luke Stock, a cattle-dealer from Wigton.

V

It was three weeks since he had fetched his flock down from the fell.

After dinner he and his mother sat together in the parlour: they had done so every Sunday afternoon, year in and year out, as far back as he could remember.

A row of mahogany chairs, with shiny, horse-hair seats, were ranged round the room. A great collection of agricultural prize-tickets were pinned over the wall; and, on a heavy, highly-polished sideboard stood several silver cups. A heap of gilt-edged shavings filled the unused grate: there were gaudily-tinted roses along the mantelpiece, and, on a small table by the window, beneath a glass-case, a gilt basket filled with imitation flowers. Every object was disposed with a scrupulous precision: the carpet and the red-patterned cloth on the centre table were much faded. The room was spotlessly clean, and wore, in the chilly winter sunlight, a rigid, comfortless air.

Neither spoke, or appeared conscious of the other's presence. Old Mrs. Garstin, wrapped in a woollen shawl, sat knitting: Anthony dozed fitfully on a stiff-backed chair.

Of a sudden, in the distance, a bell started tolling. Anthony rubbed his eyes drowsily, and taking from the table his Sunday hat, strolled out across the dusky fields. Presently, reaching a rude wooden seat, built beside the bridle-path, he sat down and relit his pipe. The air was very still; below him a white filmy mist hung across the valley: the fell-sides, vaguely grouped, resembled hulking masses of sombre shadow; and, as he looked back, three squares of glimmering gold revealed the lighted windows of the square-towered church.

He sat smoking; pondering, with placid and reverential contemplation, on the Mighty Maker of the world—a world majestically and inevitably ordered; a world where, he argued, each object—each fissure in the fells, the winding course of each tumbling stream—possesses its mysterious purport, its inevitable signification....

At the end of the field two rams were fighting; retreating, then running together, and, leaping from the ground, butting head to head and horn to horn. Anthony watched them absently, pursuing his rude meditations.

... And the succession of bad seasons, the slow ruination of the farmers throughout the country, were but punishment meted out for the accumulated wickedness of the world. In the olden time God rained plagues upon the land: nowadays, in His wrath, He spoiled the produce of the earth, which, with His own hands, He had fashioned and bestowed upon men.

He rose and continued his walk along the bridle-path. A multitude of rabbits scuttled up the hill at his approach; and a great cloud of plovers, rising from the rushes, circled overhead, filling the air with a profusion of their querulous cries. All at once he heard a rattling of stones, and perceived a number of small pieces of shingle bounding in front of him down the grassy slope.

A woman's figure was moving among the rocks above him. The next moment, by the trimming of crimson velvet on her hat, he had recognized her. He mounted the slope with springing strides, wondering the while how it was she came to be there, that she was not in church playing the organ at afternoon service.

Before she was aware of his approach, he was beside her.

'I thought ye'd be in church——' he began.

She started: then, gradually regaining her composure, answered, weakly smiling:

'Mr. Jenkinson, the new schoolmaster, wanted to try the organ.'

He came towards her impulsively: she saw the odd flickers in his eyes as she stepped back in dismay.

'Nay, but I will na harm ye,' he said. 'Only I reckon what 'tis a special turn o' Providence, meetin' wi' ye oop here. I reckon what ye'll hev t' give me a square answer noo. Ye canna dilly-dally everlastingly.'

He spoke almost brutally; and she stood, white and gasping, staring at him with large, frightened eyes. The sheep-walk was but a tiny threadlike track: the slope of the shingle on either side was very steep: below them lay the valley; distant, lifeless, all blurred by the evening dusk. She looked about her helplessly for a means of escape.

'Miss Rosa,' he continued, in a husky voice, 'can ye na coom t' think on me? Think ye, I've bin waitin' nigh upon two year for ye. I've watched ye tak oop, first wi' this young fellar, and then wi' that, till soomtimes my heart's fit t' burst. Many a day, oop on t' fell-top, t' thought o' ye's nigh driven me daft, and I've left my shepherdin' jest t' set on a cairn in t' mist, picturin' an' broodin' on yer face. Many an evenin' I've started oop t' vicarage, wi' t' resolution t' speak right oot t' ye; but when it coomed t' point, a sort o' timidity seemed t' hould me back, I was that feared t' displease ye. I knaw I'm na scholar, an' mabbe ye think I'm rough-mannered. I knaw I've spoken sharply to ye once or twice lately. But it's jest because I'm that mad wi' love for ye: I jest canna help myself soomtimes—'

He waited, peering into her face. She could see the beads of sweat above his bristling eyebrows: the damp had settled on his sandy beard: his horny fingers were twitching at the buttons of his black Sunday coat.

She struggled to summon a smile; but her under-lip quivered, and her large dark eyes filled slowly with tears.

And he went on:

'Ye've coom t' mean jest everything to me. Ef ye will na hev me, I care for nought else. I canna speak t' ye in phrases: I'm jest a plain, unscholarly man: I canna wheedle ye, wi' cunnin' after t' fashion o' toon folks. But I can love ye wi' all my might, an' watch over ye, and work for ye better than any one o' em—'

She was crying to herself, silently, while he spoke. He noticed nothing, however: the twilight hid her face from him.

'There's nought against me,' he persisted. 'I'm as good a man as any one on 'em. Ay, as good a man as any one on 'em,' he repeated defiantly, raising his voice.

'It's impossible, Mr. Garstin, it's impossible. Ye've been very kind to me—' she added, in a choking voice.

'Wa dang it, I didna mean t' mak ye cry, lass,' he exclaimed, with a softening of his tone. 'There's nought for ye t' cry ower.'

She sank on to the stones, passionately sobbing in hysterical and defenceless despair. Anthony stood a moment, gazing at her in clumsy perplexity: then, coming close to her, put his hand on her shoulder, and said gently:

'Coom, lass, what's trouble? Ye can trust me.'

She shook her head faintly.

'Ay, but ye can though,' he asserted, firmly. 'Come, what is't?'

Heedless of him, she continued to rock herself to and fro, crooning in her distress:

'Oh! I wish I were dead!... I wish I could die!'

—'Wish ye could die?' he repeated. 'Why, whatever can't be that's troublin' ye like this? There, there, lassie, give ower: it 'ull all coom right, whatever it be—'

'No, no,' she wailed. 'I wish I could die!... I wish I could die!'

Lights were twinkling in the village below; and across the valley darkness was draping the hills. The girl lifted her face from her hands, and looked up at him with a scared, bewildered expression.

'I must go home: I must be getting home,' she muttered.

'Nay, but there's sommut mighty amiss wi' ye.'

'No, it's nothing... I don't know—I'm not well... I mean it's nothing... it'll pass over... you mustn't think anything of it.'

'Nay, but I canna stand by an see ye in sich trouble.'

'It's nothing, Mr. Garstin, indeed it's nothing,' she repeated.

'Ay, but I canna credit that,' he objected stubbornly.

She sent him a shifting, hunted glance.

'Let me get home... you must let me get home.'

She made a tremulous, pitiful attempt at firmness. Eyeing her keenly, he barred her path: she flushed scarlet, and looked hastily away across the valley.

'If ye'll tell me yer distress, mabbe I can help ye.'

'No, no, it's nothing... it's nothing.'

'If ye'll tell me yer distress, mabbe I can help ye,' he repeated, with a solemn, deliberate sternness. She shivered, and looked away again, vaguely, across the valley.

'You can do nothing: there's nought to be done,' she murmured drearily.

'There's a man in this business,' he declared.

'Let me go! Let me go!' she pleaded desperately.

'Who is't that's bin puttin' ye into this distress?' His voice sounded loud and harsh.

'No one, no one. I canna tell ye, Mr. Garstin.... It's no one,' she protested weakly. The white, twisted look on his face frightened her.

'My God!' he burst out, gripping her wrist, 'an' a proper soft fool ye've made o' me. Who is't, I tell ye? Who's t' man?'

'Ye're hurtin' me. Let me go. I canna tell ye.'

'And ye're fond o' him?'

'No, no. He's a wicked, sinful man. I pray God I may never set eyes on him again. I told him so.'

'But ef he's got ye into trouble, he'll hev t' marry ye,' he persisted with a brutal bitterness.

'I will not. I hate him!' she cried fiercely.

'But is he *willin'* t' marry ye?'

'I don't know ... I don't care ... he said so before he went away ... But I'd kill myself sooner than live with him.'

He let her hands fall and stepped back from her. She could only see his figure, like a sombre cloud, standing before her. The whole fell-side seemed still and dark and lonely. Presently she heard his voice again:

'I reckon what there's one road oot o' yer distress.'

She shook her head drearily.

'There's none. I'm a lost woman.'

'An' ef ye took me instead?' he said eagerly.

'I—I don't understand—'

'Ef ye married me instead of Luke Stock?'

'But that's impossible—the—the—'

'Ay, t' child. I know. But I'll tak t' child as mine.'

She remained silent. After a moment he heard her voice answer in a queer, distant tone:

'You mean that—that ye're ready to marry me, and adopt the child?'

'I do,' he answered doggedly.

'But people—your mother—?'

'Folks 'ull jest know nought about it. It's none o' their business. T' child 'ull pass as mine. Ye'll accept that?'

'Yes,' she answered, in a low, rapid voice.

'Ye'll consent t' hev me, ef I git ye oot o' yer trouble?'

'Yes,' she repeated, in the same tone.

She heard him draw a long breath.

'I said 't was a turn o' Providence, meetin' wi' ye oop here,' he exclaimed, with half-suppressed exultation.

Her teeth began to chatter a little: she felt that he was peering at her, curiously, through the darkness.

'An' noo,' he continued briskly, 'ye'd best be gettin' home. Give me ye're hand, an' I'll stiddy ye ower t' stones.'

He helped her down the bank of shingle, exclaiming: 'By goom, ye're stony cauld.' Once or twice she slipped: he supported her, roughly gripping her knuckles. The stones rolled down the steps, noisily, disappearing into the night.

Presently they struck the turf bridle-path, and, as they descended silently towards the lights of the village, he said gravely:

'I always reckoned what my day 'ud coom.'

She made no reply; and he added grimly:

'There'll be terrible work wi' mother over this.'

He accompanied her down the narrow lane that led past her uncle's house. When the lighted windows came in sight he halted.

'Good night, lassie,' he said kindly. 'Do ye give ower distressin' yeself.'

'Good night, Mr. Garstin,' she answered, in the same low, rapid voice in which she had given him her answer up on the fell.

'We're man an' wife plighted now, are we not?' he blurted timidly.

She held her face to his, and he kissed her on the cheek, clumsily.

VI

The next morning the frost had set in. The sky was still clear and glittering: the whitened fields sparkled in the chilly sunlight: here and there, on high, distant peaks, gleamed dainty caps of snow. All the week Anthony was to be busy at the fell-foot, wall-building against the coming of the winter storms: the work was heavy, for he was single-handed, and the stone had to be fetched from off the fell-side. Two or three times a day he led his rickety, lumbering cart along the lane that passed the vicarage gate, pausing on each journey to glance furtively up at the windows. But he saw no sign of Rosa Blencarn; and, indeed, he felt no longing to see her: he was grimly exultant over the remembrance of his wooing of her, and over the knowledge that she was his. There glowed within him a stolid pride in himself: he thought of the others who had courted her, and the means by which he had won her seemed to him a fine stroke of cleverness.

And so he refrained from any mention of the matter; relishing, as he worked, all alone, the days through, the consciousness of his secret triumph, and anticipating, with inward chucklings, the discomforted cackle of his mother's female friends. He foresaw without misgiving, her bitter opposition: he felt himself strong; and his heart warmed towards the girl. And when, at intervals, the brusque realization that, after all, he was to possess her swept over him, he gripped the stones, and swung them almost fiercely into their places.

All around him the white, empty fields seemed slumbering breathlessly. The stillness stiffened the leafless trees. The frosty air flicked his blood: singing vigorously to himself he worked with a stubborn, unflagging resolution, methodically postponing, till the length of the wall should be completed, the announcement of his betrothal.

After his reticent, solitary fashion, he was very happy, reviewing his future prospects, with a plain and steady assurance, and, as the week-end approached, coming to ignore the irregularity of the whole business: almost to assume, in the exaltation of his pride, that he had won her honestly; and to discard, stolidly, all thought of Luke Stock, of his relations with her, of the coming child that was to pass for his own.

And there were moments too, when, as he sauntered homewards through the dusk at the end of his day's work, his heart grew full to overflowing of a rugged, superstitious gratitude towards God in Heaven who had granted his desires.

About three o'clock on the Saturday afternoon he finished the length of wall. He went home, washed, shaved, put on his Sunday coat; and, avoiding the kitchen, where his mother sat knitting by the fireside, strode up to the vicarage.

It was Rosa who opened the door to him. On recognizing him she started, and he followed her into the dining-room. He seated himself, and began, brusquely:

'I've coom, Miss Rosa, t' speak t' Mr. Blencarn.'

Then added, eyeing her closely:

'Ye're lookin' sick, lass.'

Her faint smile accentuated the worn, white look on her face.

'I reckon ye've been frettin' yeself,' he continued gently, 'leein' awake o' nights, hev'n't yee, noo?'

She smiled vaguely.

'Well, but ye see I've coom t' settle t' whole business for ye. Ye thought mabbe that I was na a man o' my word.'

'No, no, not that,' she protested, 'but—but—'

'But what then?'

'Ye must not do it, Mr. Garstin ... I must just bear my own trouble the best I can—' she broke out.

'D'ye fancy I'm takin' ye oot of charity? Ye little reckon the sort o' stuff my love for ye's made of. Nay, Miss Rosa, but ye canna draw back noo.'

'But ye cannot do it, Mr. Garstin. Ye know your mother will na have me at Hootsey.... I could na live there with your mother.... I'd sooner bear my trouble alone, as best I can.... She's that stern is Mrs. Garstin. I couldn't look her in the face.... I can go away somewhere.... I could keep it all from uncle.'

Her colour came and went: she stood before him, looking away from him, dully, out of the window.

'I intend ye t' coom t' Hootsey. I'm na lad: I reckon I can choose my own wife. Mother'll hev ye at t' farm, right enough: ye need na distress yeself on that point—'

'Nay, Mr. Garstin, but indeed she will not, never... I know she will not... She always set herself against me, right from the first.'

'Ay, but that was different. T' case is all changed noo,' he objected doggedly.

'She'll support the sight of me all the less,' the girl faltered.

'Mother'll hev ye at Hootsey—receive ye willin' of her own free wish—of her own free wish, d'ye hear? I'll answer for that.'

He struck the table with his fist heavily. His tone of determination awed her: she glanced at him hurriedly, struggling with her irresolution.

'I knaw hoo t' manage mother. An' now,' he concluded, changing his tone, 'is yer uncle about t' place?'

'He's up the paddock, I think,' she answered.

'Well, I'll jest step oop and hev a word wi' him.'

'Ye're ... ye will na tell him.'

'Tut, tut, na harrowin' tales, ye need na fear, lass. I reckon ef I can tackle mother, I can accommodate myself t' parson Blencarn.'

He rose, and coming close to her, scanned her face.

'Ye must git t' roses back t' yer cheeks,' he exclaimed, with a short laugh, 'I canna be takin' a ghost t' church.'

She smiled tremulously, and he continued, laying one hand affectionately on her shoulder:

'Nay, but I was but jestin'. Roses or na roses, ye'll be t' bonniest bride in all Coomberland. I'll meet ye in Hullam lane, after church time, tomorrow,' he added, moving towards the door.

After he had gone, she hurried to the backdoor furtively. His retreating figure was already mounting the grey upland field. Presently, beyond him, she perceived her uncle, emerging through the paddock gate. She ran across the poultry yard, and mounting a tub, stood watching the two figures as they moved towards one another along the brow, Anthony vigorously trudging, with his hands thrust deep in his pockets; her uncle, his wideawake tilted over his nose, hobbling, and leaning stiffly on his pair of sticks. They met; she saw Anthony take her uncle's arm: the two, turning together, strolled away towards the fell.

She went back into the house. Anthony's dog came towards her, slinking along the passage. She caught the animal's head in her hands, and bent over it caressingly, in an impulsive outburst of almost hysterical affection.

VII

The two men returned towards the vicarage. At the paddock gate they halted, and the old man concluded:

'I could not have wished a better man for her, Anthony. Mabbe the Lord'll not be minded to spare me much longer. After I'm gone Rosa'll hev all I possess. She was my poor brother Isaac's only child. After her mother was taken, he, poor fellow, went altogether to the bad, and until she came here she mostly lived among strangers. It's been a wretched sort of childhood for her—a wretched sort of childhood. Ye'll take care of her, Anthony, will ye not? ... Nay, but I could not hev wished for a better man for her, and there's my hand on 't.'

'Thank ee, Mr. Blencarn, thank ee,' Anthony answered huskily, gripping the old man's hand.

And he started off down the lane homewards.

His heart was full of a strange, rugged exaltation. He felt with a swelling pride that God had entrusted to him this great charge—to tend her; to make up to her, tenfold, for all that loving care, which, in her childhood, she had never known. And together with a stubborn confidence in himself, there welled up within him a great pity for her—a tender pity, that, chastening with his passion, made her seem to him, as he brooded over that lonely childhood of hers, the more distinctly beautiful, the more profoundly precious. He pictured to himself, tremulously, almost incredulously, their married life—in the winter, his return home at nightfall to find her awaiting him with a glad, trustful smile; their evenings, passed together, sitting in silent happiness over the smouldering logs; or, in summer-time, the midday rest in the hay-fields when, wearing perhaps a large-brimmed hat fastened with a red ribbon, beneath her chin, he would catch sight of her, carrying his dinner, coming across the upland.

She had not been brought up to be a farmer's wife: she was but a child still, as the old parson had said. She should not have to work as other men's wives worked: she should dress like a lady, and on Sundays, in church, wear fine bonnets, and remain, as she had always been, the belle of all the parish.

And, meanwhile, he would farm as he had never farmed before, watching his opportunities, driving cunning bargains, spending nothing on himself, hoarding every penny that she might have what she wanted.... And, as he strode through the village, he seemed to foresee a general brightening of prospects, a sobering of the fever of speculation in sheep, a cessation of the insensate glutting, year after year, of the great winter marts throughout the North, a slackening of the foreign competition followed by a steady revival of the price of fatted stocks—a period of prosperity in store for the farmer at last.... And the future years appeared to open out before him, spread like a distant, glittering plain, across which, he and she, hand in hand, were called to travel together....

And then, suddenly, as his iron-bound boots clattered over the cobbled yard, he remembered, with brutal determination, his mother, and the stormy struggle that awaited him.

He waited till supper was over, till his mother had moved from the table to her place by the chimney corner. For several minutes he remained debating with himself the best method of breaking the news to her. Of a sudden he glanced up at her: her knitting had slipped on to her lap: she was sitting, bunched of a heap in her chair, nodding with sleep. By the flickering light of the wood fire, she looked worn and broken: he felt a twinge of clumsy compunction. And then he remembered the piteous, hunted look in the girl's eyes, and the old man's words when they had parted at the paddock gate, and he blurted out:

'I doot but what I'll hev t' marry Rosa Blencarn after all.'

She started, and blinking her eyes, said:

'I was jest takin' a wink o' sleep. What was 't ye were saying, Tony?'

He hesitated a moment, puckering his forehead into coarse rugged lines, and fidgeting noisily with his tea-cup. Presently he repeated:

'I doot but what I'll hev t' marry Rosa Blencarn after all.'

She rose stiffly, and stepping down from the hearth, came towards him.

'Mabbe I did na hear ye aright, Tony.' She spoke hurriedly, and though she was quite close to him, steadying herself with one hand clutching the back of his chair, her voice sounded weak, distant almost.

'Look oop at me. Look oop into my face,' she commanded fiercely.

He obeyed sullenly.

'Noo oot wi 't. What's yer meanin', Tony?'

'I mean what I say,' he retorted doggedly, averting his gaze.

'What d'ye mean by sayin' that ye've *got* t' marry her?'

'I tell yer I mean what I say,' he repeated dully.

'Ye mean ye've bin an' put t' girl in trouble?'

He said nothing; but sat staring stupidly at the floor.

'Look oop at me, and answer,' she commanded, gripping his shoulder and shaking him.

He raised his face slowly, and met her glance.

'Ay, that's aboot it,' he answered.

'This'll na be truth. It'll be jest a piece o' wanton trickery!' she cried.

'Nay, but 't is truth,' he answered deliberately.

'Ye will na swear t' it?' she persisted.

'I see na necessity for swearin'.'

'Then ye canna swear t' it,' she burst out triumphantly.

He paused an instant; then said quietly:

'Ay, but I'll swear t' it easy enough. Fetch t' Book.'

She lifted the heavy, tattered Bible from the chimney-piece, and placed it before him on the table. He laid his lumpish fist on it.

'Say,' she continued with a tense tremulousness, 'say, I swear t' ye, mother, that 't is t' truth, t' whole truth, and noat but t' truth, s'help me God.'

'I swear t' ye, mother, it's truth, t' whole truth, and nothin' but t' truth, s'help me God,' he repeated after her.

'Kiss t' Book,' she ordered.

He lifted the Bible to his lips. As he replaced it on the table, he burst out into a short laugh:

'Be ye satisfied noo?'

She went back to the chimney corner without a word. The logs on the hearth hissed and crackled. Outside, amid the blackness the wind was rising, hooting through the firs, and past the windows.

After a long while he roused himself, and drawing his pipe from his pocket almost steadily, proceeded leisurely to pare in the palm of his hand a lump of black tobacco.

'We'll be asked in church Sunday,' he remarked bluntly.

She made no answer.

He looked across at her.

Her mouth was drawn tight at the corners: her face wore a queer, rigid aspect. She looked, he thought, like a figure of stone.

'Ye're not feeling poorly, are ye, mother?' he asked.

She shook her head grimly: then, hobbling out into the room, began to speak in a shrill, tuneless voice.

'Ye talked at one time o' takin' a farm over Scarsdale way. But ye'd best stop here. I'll no hinder ye. Ye can have t' large bedroom in t' front, and I'll move ower to what used to be my brother Jake's room. Ye knaw I've never had no opinion of t' girl, but I'll do what's right by her, ef I break my sperrit in t' doin' on't. I'll mak' t' girl welcome here: I'll stand by her proper-like: mebbe I'll finish by findin' soom good in her. But from this day forward, Tony, ye're na son o' mine. Ye've dishonoured yeself: ye've laid a trap for me—ay, laid a trap, that's t' word. Ye've brought shame and bitterness on yer ould mother in her ould age. Ye've made me despise t' varra sect o' ye. Ye can stop on here, but ye shall niver touch a penny of my money; every shillin' of 't shall go t' yer child, or to your child's children. Ay,' she went on, raising her voice, 'ay, ye've got yer way at last, and mebbe ye reckon ye've chosen a mighty smart way. But time 'ull coom when ye'll regret this day, when ye eat oot yer repentance in doost an' ashes. Ay, Lord 'ull punish ye, Tony, chastize ye properly. Ye'll learn that marriage begun in sin can end in nought but sin. Ay,' she concluded, as she reached the door, raising her skinny hand prophetically, 'ay, after I'm deed and gone, ye mind ye o' t' words o' t' apostle For them that hev sinned without t' law, shall also perish without t' law.'"

And she slammed the door behind her.

***

A LITTLE GREY GLOVE

By George Egerton (Mary Chavelita [Dunne] Bright)

(*Keynotes*, London: Elkin Mathews and John Lane, Vigo Street, 1893)
Early-Spring, 1893

*The book of life begins with a man and woman in a garden and
ends—with Revelations.*

OSCAR WILDE

Yes, most fellows' book of life may be said to begin at the chapter where woman comes in; mine did. She came in years ago, when I was a raw undergraduate. With the sober thought of retrospective analysis, I may say she was not all my fancy painted her; indeed now that I come to think of it there was no fancy about the vermeil of her cheeks, rather an artificial reality; she had her bower in the bar of the Golden Boar, and I was madly in love with her, seriously intent on lawful wedlock. Luckily for me she threw me over for a neighbouring pork butcher, but at the time I took it hardly, and it made me sex-shy. I was a very poor man in those days. One feels one's griefs more keenly then, one hasn't the wherewithal to buy distraction. Besides, ladies snubbed me rather, on the rare occasions I met them. Later I fell in for a legacy, the forerunner of several; indeed, I may say I am beastly rich. My tastes are simple too, and I haven't any poor relations. I believe they are of great assistance in getting rid of superfluous capital, wish I had some! It was after the legacy that women discovered my attractions. They found that there was something superb in my plainness (before, they said ugliness), something after the style of the late Victor Emanuel, something infinitely more striking than mere ordinary beauty. At least so Harding told me his sister said, and she had the reputation of being a clever girl. Being an only child, I never had the opportunity other fellows had of studying the undress side of women through familiar intercourse, say with sisters. Their most ordinary belongings were sacred to me. I had, I used to be told, ridiculous high-flown notions about them (by the way I modified those considerably on closer acquaintance). I ought to study them, nothing like a woman for developing a fellow. So I laid in a stock of books in different languages, mostly novels, in which women played title roles, in order to get up some definite data before venturing amongst them. I can't say I derived much benefit from this course. There seemed to be as great a diversity of opinion about the female species as, let us say, about the salmonidae.

My friend Ponsonby Smith, who is one of the oldest fly-fishers in the three kingdoms, said to me once: Take my word for it, there are only four true salmo; the salar, the trutta, the fario, the ferox; all the rest are just varieties, subgenuses of the above; stick to that. Some writing fellow divided all the women into good-uns and bad-uns. But as a conscientious stickler for truth, I must say that both in trout as in women, I have found myself faced with most puzzling varieties, that were a tantalizing blending of several qualities. I then resolved to study them on my own account. I pursued the Eternal Feminine in a spirit of purely scientific investigation. I knew you'd laugh sceptically at that, but it's a fact. I was impartial in my selection of subjects for observation—French, German, Spanish, as well as the home product. Nothing in petticoats escaped me. I devoted myself to the freshest *ingenue* as well as the experienced widow of three departed; and I may as well confess that the more I saw of her, the less I understood her. But I think they understood me. They refused to take me *au sérieux*. When they weren't fleecing me, they were interested in the state of my soul (I preferred the former), but all humbugged me equally, so I gave them up. I took to rod and gun instead, *pro salute animae*; it's decidedly safer. I have scoured every country in the globe; indeed I can say that I have shot and fished in woods and waters where no other white man, perhaps ever dropped a beast or played a fish before. There is no life like the life of a free wanderer, and no lore like the lore one gleans in the great book of nature. But one must have freed one's spirit from the taint of the town before one can even read the alphabet of its mystic meaning.

What has this to do with the glove? True, not much, and yet it has a connection—it accounts for me.

Well, for twelve years I have followed the impulses of the wandering spirit that dwells in me. I have seen the sun rise in Finland and gild the Devil's Knuckles as he sank behind the Drachensberg. I have caught the barba and the gamer yellow fish in the Vaal river, taken muskelunge and black-bass in Canada, thrown a fly over *guapote* and *cavallo* in Central American lakes, and choked the monster eels of the Mauritius with a cunningly faked-up duckling. But I have been shy as a chub at the shadow of a woman.

Well, it happened last year I came back on business—another confounded legacy; end of June too, just as I was off to Finland. But Messrs. Thimble and Rigg, the highly respectable firm who look after my affairs, represented that I owed it to others, whom I kept out of their share of the legacy, to stay near town till affairs were wound up. They told me, with a view to reconcile me perhaps, of a trout stream with a decent inn near it; an unknown stream in Kent. It seems a junior member of the firm is an angler, at least he sometimes catches pike or perch in the Medway some way from the stream where the trout rise in audacious security from artificial lures. I stipulated for a clerk to come down with any papers to be signed, and started at once for Victoria. I decline to tell the name of my find, firstly because the trout are the gamest little fish that ever rose to fly and run to a good two pounds. Secondly, I have paid for all the rooms in the inn for the next year, and I want it to myself. The glove is lying on the table next me as I write. If it isn't in my breast-pocket or under my pillow, it is in some place where I can see it. It has a delicate grey body (suède, I think they call it) with a whipping of silver round the top, and a darker grey silk tag to fasten it. It is marked 5-3/4 inside, and has a delicious scent about it, to keep off moths, I suppose; naphthaline is better. It reminds me of a 'silver-sedge' tied on a ten hook. I startled the good landlady of the little inn (there is no village fortunately) when I arrived with the only porter of the tiny station laden with traps. She hesitated about a private sitting-room, but eventually we compromised matters, as I was willing to share it with the other visitor. I got into knickerbockers at once, collared a boy to get me worms and minnow for the morrow, and as I felt too lazy to unpack tackle, just sat in the shiny armchair (made comfortable by the successive sitting of former occupants) at the open window and looked out. The river, not the trout stream, winds to the right, and the trees cast trembling shadows into its clear depths. The red tiles of a farm roof show between the beeches, and break the monotony of blue sky background. A dusty waggoner is slaking his thirst with a tankard of ale. I am conscious of the strange lonely feeling that a visit to England always gives me. Away in strange lands, even in solitary places, one doesn't feel it somehow. One is filled with the hunter's lust, bent on a 'kill', but at home in the quiet country, with the smoke curling up from some fireside, the mowers busy laying the hay in swaths, the children tumbling under the trees in the orchards, and a girl singing as she spreads the clothes on the sweetbriar hedge, amidst a scene quick with home sights and sounds, a strange lack creeps in and makes itself felt in a dull, aching way. Oddly enough, too, I had a sense of uneasiness, a 'something going to happen'. I had often experienced it when out alone in a great forest, or on an unknown lake, and it always meant 'ware danger' of some kind. But why should I feel it here? Yet I did, and I couldn't shake it off. I took to examining the room. It was a commonplace one of the usual type. But there was a work-basket on the table, a dainty thing, lined with blue satin. There was a bit of lace stretched over shiny blue linen, with the needle sticking in it; such fairy work, like cobwebs seen from below, spun from a branch against a background of sky. A gold thimble, too, with initials, not the landlady's, I know. What pretty things, too, in the basket! A scissors, a capital shape for fly-making; a little file, and some floss silk and tinsel, the identical colour I want for a new fly I have in my head, one that will be a demon to kill. The northern devil I mean to call him. Some one looks in behind me, and a light step passes upstairs. I drop the basket, I don't know why. There are some reviews near it. I take up one, and am soon buried in an article on Tasmanian fauna. It is strange, but whenever I do know anything about a subject, I always find these writing fellows either entirely ignorant or damned wrong.

After supper, I took a stroll to see the river. It was a silver grey evening, with just the last lemon and pink streaks of the sunset staining the sky. There had been a shower, and somehow the smell of the dust after rain mingled with the mignonette in the garden brought back vanished scenes of small-boyhood, when I caught minnows in a bottle, and dreamt of a shilling rod as happiness unattainable. I turned aside from the road in accordance with directions, and walked towards the stream. Holloa! someone before me, what a bore! The angler is hidden by an elder-bush, but I can see the fly drop delicately, artistically on the water. Fishing upstream, too! There is a bit of broken water there, and the midges dance in myriads; a silver gleam, and the line spins out, and the fly falls just in the right place. It is growing dusk, but the fellow is an adept at quick, fine casting—I wonder what fly he has on—why, he's going to try downstream now? I hurry forward, and as I near him, I swerve to the left out of the way. S-s-s-s! a sudden sting in the lobe of my ear. Hey! I cry as I find I am caught; the tail fly is fast in it. A slight, grey-clad woman holding the rod lays it carefully down and comes towards me through the gathering dusk. My first impulse is to snap the gut and take to my heels, but I am held by something less tangible but far more powerful than the grip of the Limerick hook in my ear.

'I am very sorry!' she says in a voice that matched the evening, it was so quiet and soft; 'but it was exceedingly stupid of you to come behind like that.'

'I didn't think you threw such a long line; I thought I was safe,' I stammered.

'Hold this!' she says, giving me a diminutive fly-book, out of which she has taken a scissors. I obey meekly. She snips the gut.

'Have you a sharp knife? If I strip the hook you can push it through; it is lucky it isn't in the cartilage.'

I suppose I am an awful idiot, but I only handed her the knife, and she proceeded as calmly as if stripping a hook in a man's ear were an everyday occurrence. Her gown is of some soft grey stuff, and her grey leather belt is silver clasped. Her hands are soft and cool and steady, but there is a rarely disturbing thrill in their gentle touch. The thought flashed through my mind that I had just missed that, a woman's voluntary tender touch, not a paid caress, all my life.

'Now you can push it through yourself. I hope it won't hurt much.' Taking the hook, I push it through, and a drop of blood follows it. 'Oh!' she cries, but I assure her it is nothing, and stick the hook surreptitiously in my coat sleeve. Then we both laugh, and I look at her for the first time. She has a very white forehead, with little tendrils of hair blowing round it under her grey cap, her eyes are grey. I didn't see that then, I only saw they were steady, smiling eyes that matched her mouth. Such a mouth, the most maddening mouth a man ever longed to kiss, above a too-pointed chin, soft as a child's; indeed, the whole face looks soft in the misty light.

'I am sorry I spoilt your sport!' I say.

'Oh, that don't matter, it's time to stop. I got two brace, one a beauty.'

She is winding in her line, and I look in her basket; they *are* beauties, one two-pounder, the rest running from a half to a pound.

'What fly?'

'Yellow dun took that one, but your assailant was a partridge spider.' I sling her basket over my shoulder; she takes it as a matter of course, and we retrace our steps. I feel curiously happy as we walk towards the road; there is a novel delight in her nearness; the feel of woman works subtly and strangely in me; the rustle of her skirt as it brushes the black-heads in the meadow-grass, and the delicate perfume, partly violets, partly herself, that comes to me with each of her movements is a rare pleasure. I am hardly surprised when she turns into the garden of the inn, I think I knew from the first that she would.

'Better bathe that ear of yours, and put a few drops of carbolic in the water.' She takes the basket as she says it, and goes into the kitchen. I hurry over this, and go into the little sitting-room. There is a tray with a glass of milk and some oaten cakes upon the table. I am too disturbed to sit down; I stand at the window and watch the bats flitter in the gathering moonlight, and listen with quivering nerves for her step—

perhaps she will send for the tray, and not come after all. What a fool I am to be disturbed by a grey-clad witch with a tantalizing mouth! That comes of loafing about doing nothing. I mentally darn the old fool who saved her money instead of spending it. Why the devil should I be bothered? I don't want it anyhow. She comes in as I fume, and I forget everything at her entrance. I push the armchair towards the table, and she sinks quietly into it, pulling the tray nearer. She has a wedding ring on, but somehow it never strikes me to wonder if she is married or a widow or who she may be. I am content to watch her break her biscuits. She has the prettiest hands, and a trick of separating her last fingers when she takes hold of anything. They remind me of white orchids I saw somewhere. She led me to talk; about Africa, I think. I liked to watch her eyes glow deeply in the shadow and then catch light as she bent forward to say something in her quick responsive way.

'Long ago when I was a girl,' she said once.

'Long ago?' I echo incredulously, 'surely not?'

'Ah, but yes, you haven't seen me in the daylight,' with a soft little laugh. 'Do you know what the gipsies say? "Never judge a woman or a ribbon by candle-light." They might have said moonlight equally well.'

She rises as she speaks, and I feel an overpowering wish to have her put out her hand. But she does not, she only takes the work-basket and a book, and says good night with an inclination of her little head.

I go over and stand next to her chair; I don't like to sit in it, but I like to put my hand where her head leant, and fancy, if she were there, how she would look up.

I woke next morning with a curious sense of pleasurable excitement. I whistled from very lightness of heart as I dressed. When I got down I found the landlady clearing away her breakfast things. I felt disappointed and resolved to be down earlier in future. I didn't feel inclined to try the minnow. I put them in a tub in the yard and tried to read and listen for her step. I dined alone. The day dragged terribly. I did not like to ask about her, I had a notion she might not like it. I spent the evening on the river. I might have filled a good basket, but I let the beggars rest. After all, I had caught fish enough to stock all the rivers in Great Britain.

There are other things than trout in the world. I sit and smoke a pipe where she caught me last night. If I half close my eyes I can see hers, and her mouth, in the smoke. That is one of the curious charms of baccy, it helps to reproduce brain pictures. After a bit, I think 'perhaps she has left'. I get quite feverish at the thought and hasten back. I must ask. I look up at the window as I pass; there is surely a gleam of white. I throw down my traps and hasten up. She is leaning with her arms on the window-ledge staring out into the gloom. I could swear I caught a suppressed sob as I entered. I cough, and she turns quickly and bows slightly. A bonnet and gloves and lace affair and a lot of papers are lying on the table. I am awfully afraid she is going. I say—

'Please don't let me drive you away, it is so early yet. I half expected to see you on the river.'

'Nothing so pleasant; I have been up in town (the tears have certainly got into her voice) all day; it was so hot and dusty, I am tired out.'

The little servant brings in the lamp and a tray with a bottle of lemonade.

'Mistress hasn't any lemons, 'm, will this do?'

'Yes,' she says wearily, she is shading her eyes with her hand; 'anything; I am fearfully thirsty.'

'Let me concoct you a drink instead. I have lemons and ice and things. My man sent me down supplies today; I leave him in town. I am rather a dab at drinks; I learnt it from the Yankees; about the only thing I did learn from them I care to remember. Susan!' The little maid helps me to get the materials, and *she* watches me quietly. When I give it to her she takes it with a smile (she *has* been crying). That is an ample thank you. She looks quite old. Something more than tiredness called up those lines in her face.

Well, ten days passed, sometimes we met at breakfast, sometimes at supper, sometimes we fished together or sat in the straggling orchard and talked; she neither avoided me nor sought me. She is the most charming mixture of child and woman I ever met. She is a dual creature. Now I never met that in a man. When she is here without getting a letter in the morning or going to town, she seems like a girl. She runs about in her grey gown and little cap and laughs, and seems to throw off all thought like an irresponsible child. She is eager to fish, or pick gooseberries and eat them daintily, or sit under the trees and talk. But when she goes to town—I notice she always goes when she gets a lawyer's letter, there is no mistaking the envelope—she comes home tired and haggard-looking, an old woman of thirty-five. I wonder why. It takes her, even with her elasticity of temperament, nearly a day to get young again. I hate her to go to town; it is extraordinary how I miss her; I can't recall, when she is absent, her saying anything very wonderful, but she converses all the time. She has a gracious way of filling the place with herself, there is an entertaining quality in her very presence. We had one rainy afternoon; she tied me some flies (I shan't use any of them); I watched the lights in her hair as she moved, it is quite golden in some places, and she has a tiny mole near her left ear and another on her left wrist. On the eleventh day she got a letter but she didn't go to town, she stayed up in her room all day; twenty times I felt inclined to send her a line, but I had no excuse. I heard the landlady say as I passed the kitchen window: 'Poor dear! I'm sorry to lose her!' Lose her? I should think not. It has come to this with me that I don't care to face any future without her; and yet I know nothing about her, not even if she is a free woman. I shall find that out the next time I see her. In the evening I catch a glimpse of her gown in the orchard, and I follow her. We sit down near the river. Her left hand is lying gloveless next to me in the grass.

'Do you think from what you have seen of me, that I would ask a question out of any mere impertinent curiosity?'

She starts. 'No, I do not!'

I take up her hand and touch the ring. 'Tell me, does this bind you to any one?'

I am conscious of a buzzing in my ears and a dancing blurr of water and sky and trees, as I wait (it seems to me an hour) for her reply. I felt the same sensation once before, when I got drawn into some rapids and had an awfully narrow shave, but of that another time.

The voice is shaking.

'I am not legally bound to anyone, at least; but why do you ask?' she looks me square in the face as she speaks, with a touch of haughtiness I never saw in her before.

Perhaps the great relief I feel, the sense of joy at knowing she is free, speaks out of my face, for hers flushes and she drops her eyes, her lips tremble. I don't look at her again, but I can see her all the same. After a while she says—

'I half intended to tell you something about myself this evening, now I *must*. Let us go in. I shall come down to the sitting-room after your supper.' She takes a long look at the river and the inn, as if fixing the place in her memory; it strikes me with a chill that there is a goodbye in her gaze. Her eyes rest on me a moment as they come back, there is a sad look in their grey clearness. She swings her little grey gloves in her hand as we walk back. I can hear her walking up and down overhead; how tired she will be, and how slowly the time goes. I am standing at one side of the window when she enters; she stands at the other, leaning her head against the shutter with her hands clasped before her. I can hear my own heart beating, and, I fancy, hers through the stillness. The suspense is fearful. At length she says—

'You have been a long time out of England; you don't read the papers?'

'No.' A pause. I believe my heart is beating inside my head.

'You asked me if I was a free woman. I don't pretend to misunderstand why you asked me. I am not a beautiful woman, I never was. But there must be something about me, there is in some women, "essential femininity" perhaps, that appeals to all men. What I read in your eyes I have seen in many men's before, but before God I never tried to rouse it. Today (with a sob), I can say I am free, yesterday morning I could not. Yesterday my husband gained his case and divorced me!' she closes her eyes and draws in her under-lip to stop its quivering. I want to take her in my arms, but I am afraid to.

'I did not ask you any more than if you were free!'

'No, but I am afraid you don't quite take in the meaning. I did not divorce my husband, he divorced *me*, he got a decree *nisi*; do you understand now? (she is speaking with difficulty), do you know what that implies?'

I can't stand her face any longer. I take her hands, they are icy cold, and hold them tightly.

'Yes, I know what it implies, that is, I know the legal and social conclusion to be drawn from it—if that is what you mean. But I never asked you for that information. I have nothing to do with your past. You did not exist for me before the day we met on the river. I take you from that day and I ask you to marry me.'

I feel her tremble and her hands get suddenly warm. She turns her head and looks at me long and searchingly, then she says—

'Sit down, I want to say something!'

I obey, and she comes and stands next the chair. I can't help it, I reach up my arm, but she puts it gently down.

'No, you must listen without touching me, I shall go back to the window. I don't want to influence you a bit by any personal magnetism I possess. I want you to listen—I have told you he divorced me, the co-respondent was an old friend, a friend of my childhood, of my girlhood. He died just after the first application was made, luckily for me. He would have considered my honour before my happiness. *I* did not defend the case, it wasn't likely—ah, if you knew all? He proved his case; given clever counsel, willing witnesses to whom you make it worth while, and no defence, divorce is always attainable even in England. But remember: I figure as an adulteress in every English-speaking paper. If you buy last week's evening papers—do you remember the day I was in town?'—I nod—'you will see a sketch of me in that day's; someone, perhaps he, must have given it; it was from an old photograph. I bought one at Victoria as I came out; it is funny (with an hysterical laugh) to buy a caricature of one's own poor face at a news-stall. Yet in spite of that I have felt glad. The point for you is that I made no defence to the world, and (with a lifting of her head) I will make no apology, no explanation, no denial to you, now nor ever. I am very desolate and your attention came very warm to me, but I don't love you. Perhaps I could learn to (with a rush of colour), for what you have said tonight, and it is because of that I tell you to weigh what this means. Later, when your care for me will grow into habit, you may chafe at my past. It is from that I would save you.'

I hold out my hands and she comes and puts them aside and takes me by the beard and turns up my face and scans it earnestly. She must have

   Victorian Short Stories: Stories of Courtship

been deceived a good deal. I let her do as she pleases, it is the wisest way with women, and it is good to have her touch me in that way. She seems satisfied. She stands leaning against the arm of the chair and says—

'I must learn first to think of myself as a free woman again, it almost seems wrong today to talk like this; can you understand that feeling?'

I nod assent.

'Next time I must be sure, and you must be sure,' she lays her fingers on my mouth as I am about to protest, 'S-sh! You shall have a year to think. If you repeat then what you have said today, I shall give you your answer. You must not try to find me. I have money. If I am living, I will come here to you. If I am dead, you will be told of it. In the year between I shall look upon myself as belonging to you, and render an account if you wish of every hour. You will not be influenced by me in any way, and you will be able to reason it out calmly. If you think better of it, don't come.'

I feel there would be no use trying to move her, I simply kiss her hands and say:

'As you will, dear woman, I shall be here.'

We don't say any more; she sits down on a footstool with her head against my knee, and I just smooth it. When the clocks strike ten through the house, she rises and I stand up. I see that she has been crying quietly, poor lonely little soul. I lift her off her feet and kiss her, and stammer out my sorrow at losing her, and she is gone. Next morning the little maid brought me an envelope from the lady, who left by the first train. It held a little grey glove; that is why I carry it always, and why I haunt the inn and never leave it for longer than a week; why I sit and dream in the old chair that has a ghost of her presence always; dream of the spring to come with the May-fly on the wing, and the young summer when midges dance, and the trout are growing fastidious; when she will come to me across the meadow grass, through the silver haze, as she did before; come with her grey eyes shining to exchange herself for her little grey glove.

***

THE WOMAN BEATER

By Israel Zangwill

(The Grey Wig/Stories and Novelettes, New York: The Macmillan Company, 1903)

I

She came 'to meet John Lefolle', but John Lefolle did not know he was to meet Winifred Glamorys. He did not even know he was himself the meeting-point of all the brilliant and beautiful persons, assembled in the publisher's Saturday Salon, for although a youthful minor poet, he was modest and lovable. Perhaps his Oxford tutorship was sobering. At any rate his head remained unturned by his precocious fame, and to meet these other young men and women—his reverend seniors on the slopes of Parnassus—gave him more pleasure than the receipt of 'royalties'. Not that his publisher afforded him much opportunity of contrasting the two pleasures. The profits of the Muse went to provide this room of old furniture and roses, this beautiful garden a-twinkle with Japanese lanterns, like gorgeous fire-flowers blossoming under the white crescent-moon of early June.

Winifred Glamorys was not literary herself. She was better than a poetess, she was a poem. The publisher always threw in a few realities, and some beautiful brainless creature would generally be found the nucleus of a crowd, while Clio in spectacles languished in a corner. Winifred Glamorys, however, was reputed to have a tongue that matched her eye; paralleling with whimsies and epigrams its freakish fires and witcheries, and, assuredly, flitting in her white gown through the dark balmy garden, she seemed the very spirit of moonlight, the subtle incarnation of night and roses.

When John Lefolle met her, Cecilia was with her, and the first conversation was triangular. Cecilia fired most of the shots; she was a bouncing, rattling beauty, chockful of confidence and high spirits, except when asked to do the one thing she could do—sing! Then she became—quite genuinely—a nervous, hesitant, pale little thing. However, the suppliant hostess bore her off, and presently her rich contralto notes passed through the garden, adding to its passion and mystery, and through the open French windows, John could see her standing against the wall near the piano, her head thrown back, her eyes half-closed, her creamy throat swelling in the very abandonment of artistic ecstasy.

'What a charming creature!' he exclaimed involuntarily.

'That is what everybody thinks, except her husband,' Winifred laughed.

'Is he blind then?' asked John with his cloistral *naïveté*.

'Blind? No, love is blind. Marriage is never blind.'

The bitterness in her tone pierced John. He felt vaguely the passing of some icy current from unknown seas of experience. Cecilia's voice soared out enchantingly.

'Then, marriage must be deaf,' he said, 'or such music as that would charm it.'

She smiled sadly. Her smile was the tricksy play of moonlight among clouds of faëry.

'You have never been married,' she said simply.

'Do you mean that you, too, are neglected?' something impelled him to exclaim.

'Worse,' she murmured.

'It is incredible!' he cried. 'You!'

'Hush! My husband will hear you.'

Her warning whisper brought him into a delicious conspiracy with her. 'Which is your husband?' he whispered back.

'There! Near the casement, standing gazing open-mouthed at Cecilia. He always opens his mouth when she sings. It is like two toys moved by the same wire.'

He looked at the tall, stalwart, ruddy-haired Anglo-Saxon. 'Do you mean to say he—?'

'I mean to say nothing.'

'But you said—'

'I said "worse".'

'Why, what can be worse?'

She put her hand over her face. 'I am ashamed to tell you.' How adorable was that half-divined blush!

'But you must tell me everything.' He scarcely knew how he had leapt into this role of confessor. He only felt they were 'moved by the same wire'.

Her head drooped on her breast. 'He—beats—me.'

'What!' John forgot to whisper. It was the greatest shock his recluse life had known, compact as it was of horror at the revelation, shamed confusion at her candour, and delicious pleasure in her confidence.

This fragile, exquisite creature under the rod of a brutal bully!

Once he had gone to a wedding reception, and among the serious presents some grinning Philistine drew his attention to an uncouth club—'a wife-beater' he called it. The flippancy had jarred upon John terribly: this intrusive reminder of the customs of the slums. It grated like Billingsgate in a boudoir. Now that savage weapon recurred to him—for a lurid instant he saw Winifred's husband wielding it. Oh, abomination of his sex! And did he stand there, in his immaculate evening dress, posing as an English gentleman? Even so might some gentleman burglar bear through a salon his imperturbable swallow-tail.

Beat a woman! Beat that essence of charm and purity, God's best gift to man, redeeming him from his own grossness! Could such things be? John Lefolle would as soon have credited the French legend that English wives are sold in Smithfield. No! it could not be real that this flower-like figure was thrashed.

'Do you mean to say—?' he cried. The rapidity of her confidence alone made him feel it all of a dreamlike unreality.

'Hush! Cecilia's singing!' she admonished him with an unexpected smile, as her fingers fell from her face.

'Oh, you have been making fun of me.' He was vastly relieved. 'He beats you—at chess—or at lawn-tennis?'

'Does one wear a high-necked dress to conceal the traces of chess, or lawn-tennis?'

He had not noticed her dress before, save for its spiritual whiteness. Susceptible though he was to beautiful shoulders, Winifred's enchanting face had been sufficiently distracting. Now the thought of physical bruises gave him a second spasm of righteous horror. That delicate rose-leaf flesh abraded and lacerated!

'The ruffian! Does he use a stick or a fist?'

'Both! But as a rule he just takes me by the arms and shakes me like a terrier a rat. I'm all black and blue now.'

'Poor butterfly!' he murmured poetically.

'Why did I tell you?' she murmured back with subtler poetry.

The poet thrilled in every vein. 'Love at first sight', of which he had often read and often written, was then a reality! It could be as mutual, too, as Romeo's and Juliet's. But how awkward that Juliet should be married and her husband a Bill Sykes in broad-cloth!

II

Mrs. Glamorys herself gave 'At Homes', every Sunday afternoon, and so, on the morrow, after a sleepless night mitigated by perpended sonnets, the love-sick young tutor presented himself by invitation at the beautiful old house in Hampstead. He was enchanted to find his heart's mistress set in an eighteenth-century frame of small-paned windows and of high oak-panelling, and at once began to image her dancing minuets and playing on virginals. Her husband was absent, but a broad band of velvet round Winifred's neck was a painful reminder of his possibilities. Winifred, however, said it was only a touch of sore throat caught in the garden. Her eyes added that there was nothing in the pathological dictionary which she would not willingly have caught for the sake of those divine, if draughty moments; but that, alas! it was more than a mere bodily ailment she had caught there.

There were a great many visitors in the two delightfully quaint rooms, among whom he wandered disconsolate and admired, jealous of her scattered smiles, but presently he found himself seated by her side on a 'cosy corner' near the open folding-doors, with all the other guests huddled round a violinist in the inner room. How Winifred had managed it he did not know but she sat plausibly in the outer room, awaiting newcomers, and this particular niche was invisible, save to a determined eye. He took her unresisting hand—that dear, warm hand, with its begemmed artistic fingers, and held it in uneasy beatitude. How wonderful! She—the beautiful and adored hostess, of whose sweetness and charm he heard even her own guests murmur to one another—it was her actual flesh-and-blood hand that lay in his—thrillingly tangible. Oh, adventure beyond all merit, beyond all hoping!

But every now and then, the outer door facing them would open on some newcomer, and John had hastily to release her soft magnetic fingers and sit demure, and jealously overhear her effusive welcome to those innocent intruders, nor did his brow clear till she had shepherded them within the inner fold. Fortunately, the refreshments were in this section, so that once therein, few of the sheep strayed back, and the jiggling wail of the violin was succeeded by a shrill babble of tongues and the clatter of cups and spoons. 'Get me an ice, please—strawberry,' she ordered John during one of these forced intervals in manual flirtation; and when he had steered laboriously to and fro, he found a young actor beside her in his cosy corner, and his jealous fancy almost saw *their* hands dispart. He stood over them with a sickly smile, while Winifred ate her ice. When he returned from depositing the empty saucer, the player-fellow was gone, and in remorse for his mad suspicion he stooped and reverently lifted her fragrant finger-tips to his lips. The door behind his back opened abruptly.

'Goodbye,' she said, rising in a flash. The words had the calm conventional cadence, and instantly extorted from him—amid all his dazedness—the corresponding 'Goodbye'. When he turned and saw it was Mr. Glamorys who had come in, his heart leapt wildly at the nearness of his escape. As he passed this masked ruffian, he nodded perfunctorily and received a cordial smile. Yes, he was handsome and fascinating enough externally, this blonde savage.

'A man may smile and smile and be a villain,' John thought. 'I wonder how he'd feel, if he knew I knew he beats women.'

Already John had generalized the charge. 'I hope Cecilia will keep him at arm's length,' he had said to Winifred, 'if only that she may not smart for it some day.'

He lingered purposely in the hall to get an impression of the brute, who had begun talking loudly to a friend with irritating bursts of laughter, speciously frank-ringing. Golf, fishing, comic operas—ah, the Boeotian! These were the men who monopolized the ethereal divinities.

But this brusque separation from his particular divinity was disconcerting. How to see her again? He must go up to Oxford in the morning, he wrote her that night, but if she could possibly let him call during the week he would manage to run down again.

'Oh, my dear, dreaming poet,' she wrote to Oxford, 'how could you possibly send me a letter to be laid on the breakfast-table beside *The Times*! With a poem in it, too. Fortunately my husband was in a hurry to get down to the City, and he neglected to read my correspondence. (The unchivalrous blackguard,' John commented. 'But what can be expected of a woman beater?') Never, never write to me again at the house. A letter, care of Mrs. Best, 8A Foley Street, W.C., will always find me. She is my maid's mother. And you must not come here either, my dear handsome head-in-the-clouds, except to my 'At Homes', and then only at judicious intervals. I shall be walking round the pond in Kensington Gardens at four next Wednesday, unless Mrs. Best brings me a letter to the contrary. And now thank you for your delicious poem; I do not recognize my humble self in the dainty lines, but I shall always be proud to think I inspired them. Will it be in the new volume? I have never been in print before; it will be a novel sensation. I cannot pay you song for song, only feeling for feeling. Oh, John Lefolle, why did we not meet when I had still my girlish dreams? Now, I have grown to distrust all men—to fear the brute beneath the cavalier....'

Mrs. Best did bring her a letter, but it was not to cancel the appointment, only to say he was not surprised at her horror of the male sex, but that she must beware of false generalizations. Life was still a wonderful and beautiful thing—*vide* poem enclosed. He was counting the minutes till Wednesday afternoon. It was surely a popular mistake that only sixty went to the hour.

This chronometrical reflection recurred to him even more poignantly in the hour that he circumambulated the pond in Kensington Gardens. Had she forgotten—had her husband locked her up? What could have happened? It seemed six hundred minutes, ere, at ten past five she came tripping daintily towards him. His brain had been reduced to insanely devising problems for his pupils—if a man walks two strides of one and a half feet a second round a lake fifty acres in area, in how many turns will he overtake a lady who walks half as fast and isn't there?—but the moment her pink parasol loomed on the horizon, all his long misery vanished in an ineffable peace and uplifting. He hurried, bare-headed, to clasp her little gloved hand. He had forgotten her unpunctuality, nor did she remind him of it.

'How sweet of you to come all that way,' was all she said, and it was a sufficient reward for the hours in the train and the six hundred minutes among the nursemaids and perambulators. The elms were in their glory, the birds were singing briskly, the water sparkled, the sunlit sward stretched fresh and green—it was the loveliest, coolest moment of the afternoon. John instinctively turned down a leafy avenue. Nature and Love! What more could poet ask?

'No, we can't have tea by the Kiosk,' Mrs. Glamorys protested. 'Of course I love anything that savours of Paris, but it's become so

   Victorian Short Stories: Stories of Courtship

fashionable. There will be heaps of people who know me. I suppose you've forgotten it's the height of the season. I know a quiet little place in the High Street.' She led him, unresisting but bemused, towards the gate, and into a confectioner's. Conversation languished on the way.

'Tea,' he was about to instruct the pretty attendant.

'Strawberry ices,' Mrs. Glamorys remarked gently. 'And some of those nice French cakes.'

The ice restored his spirits, it was really delicious, and he had got so hot and tired, pacing round the pond. Decidedly Winifred was a practical person and he was a dreamer. The pastry he dared not touch—being a genius—but he was charmed at the gaiety with which Winifred crammed cake after cake into her rosebud of a mouth. What an enchanting creature! how bravely she covered up her life's tragedy!

The thought made him glance at her velvet band—it was broader than ever.

'He has beaten you again!' he murmured furiously. Her joyous eyes saddened, she hung her head, and her fingers crumbled the cake. 'What is his pretext?' he asked, his blood burning.

'Jealousy,' she whispered.

His blood lost its glow, ran cold. He felt the bully's blows on his own skin, his romance turning suddenly sordid. But he recovered his courage. He, too, had muscles. 'But I thought he just missed seeing me kiss your hand.'

She opened her eyes wide. 'It wasn't you, you darling old dreamer.'

He was relieved and disturbed in one.

'Somebody else?' he murmured. Somehow the vision of the player-fellow came up.

She nodded. 'Isn't it lucky he has himself drawn a red-herring across the track? I didn't mind his blows—*you* were safe!' Then, with one of her adorable transitions, 'I am dreaming of another ice,' she cried with roguish wistfulness.

'I was afraid to confess my own greediness,' he said, laughing. He beckoned the waitress. 'Two more.'

'We haven't got any more strawberries,' was her unexpected reply. 'There's been such a run on them today.'

Winifred's face grew overcast. 'Oh, nonsense!' she pouted. To John the moment seemed tragic.

'Won't you have another kind?' he queried. He himself liked any kind, but he could scarcely eat a second ice without her.

Winifred meditated. 'Coffee?' she queried.

The waitress went away and returned with a face as gloomy as Winifred's. 'It's been such a hot day,' she said deprecatingly. 'There is only one ice in the place and that's Neapolitan.'

'Well, bring two Neapolitans,' John ventured.

'I mean there is only one Neapolitan ice left.'

'Well, bring that. I don't really want one.'

He watched Mrs. Glamorys daintily devouring the solitary ice, and felt a certain pathos about the parti-coloured oblong, a something of the haunting sadness of 'The Last Rose of Summer'. It would make a graceful, serio-comic triolet, he was thinking. But at the last spoonful, his beautiful companion dislocated his rhymes by her sudden upspringing.

'Goodness gracious,' she cried, 'how late it is!'

'Oh, you're not leaving me yet!' he said. A world of things sprang to his brain, things that he was going to say—to arrange. They had said nothing—not a word of their love even; nothing but cakes and ices.

'Poet!' she laughed. 'Have you forgotten I live at Hampstead?' She picked up her parasol.

'Put me into a hansom, or my husband will be raving at his lonely dinner-table.'

He was so dazed as to be surprised when the waitress blocked his departure with a bill. When Winifred was spirited away, he remembered she might, without much risk, have given him a lift to Paddington. He hailed another hansom and caught the next train to Oxford. But he was too late for his own dinner in Hall.

III

He was kept very busy for the next few days, and could only exchange a passionate letter or two with her. For some time the examination fever had been raging, and in every college poor patients sat with wet towels round their heads. Some, who had neglected their tutor all the term, now strove to absorb his omniscience in a sitting.

On the Monday, John Lefolle was good-naturedly giving a special audience to a muscular dunce, trying to explain to him the political effects of the Crusades, when there was a knock at the sitting-room door, and the scout ushered in Mrs. Glamorys. She was bewitchingly dressed in white, and stood in the open doorway, smiling—an embodiment of the summer he was neglecting. He rose, but his tongue was paralysed. The dunce became suddenly important—a symbol of the decorum he had been outraging. His soul, torn so abruptly from history to romance, could not get up the right emotion. Why this imprudence of Winifred's? She had been so careful heretofore.

'What a lot of boots there are on your staircase!' she said gaily.

He laughed. The spell was broken. 'Yes, the heap to be cleaned is rather obtrusive,' he said, 'but I suppose it is a sort of tradition.'

'I think I've got hold of the thing pretty well now, sir.' The dunce rose and smiled, and his tutor realized how little the dunce had to learn in some things. He felt quite grateful to him.

'Oh, well, you'll come and see me again after lunch, won't you, if one or two points occur to you for elucidation,' he said, feeling vaguely a liar, and generally guilty. But when, on the departure of the dunce, Winifred held out her arms, everything fell from him but the sense of the exquisite moment. Their lips met for the first time, but only for an instant. He had scarcely time to realize that this wonderful thing had happened before the mobile creature had darted to his book-shelves and was examining a Thucydides upside down.

'How clever to know Greek!' she exclaimed. 'And do you really talk it with the other dons?'

'No, we never talk shop,' he laughed. 'But, Winifred, what made you come here?'

'I had never seen Oxford. Isn't it beautiful?'

'There's nothing beautiful *here*,' he said, looking round his sober study.

'No,' she admitted; 'there's nothing I care for here,' and had left another celestial kiss on his lips before he knew it. 'And now you must take me to lunch and on the river.'

He stammered, 'I have—work.'

She pouted. 'But I can't stay beyond tomorrow morning, and I want so much to see all your celebrated oarsmen practising.'

'You are not staying over the night?' he gasped.

'Yes, I am,' and she threw him a dazzling glance.

His heart went pit-a-pat. 'Where?' he murmured.

'Oh, some poky little hotel near the station. The swell hotels are full.'

He was glad to hear she was not conspicuously quartered.

'So many people have come down already for Commem,' he said. 'I suppose they are anxious to see the Generals get their degrees. But hadn't we better go somewhere and lunch?'

They went down the stone staircase, past the battalion of boots, and across the quad. He felt that all the windows were alive with eyes, but she insisted on standing still and admiring their ivied picturesqueness. After lunch he shamefacedly borrowed the dunce's punt. The necessities of punting, which kept him far from her, and demanded much adroit labour, gradually restored his self-respect, and he was able to look the uncelebrated oarsmen they met in the eyes, except when they were accompanied by their parents and sisters, which subtly made him feel uncomfortable again. But Winifred, piquant under her pink parasol, was singularly at ease, enraptured with the changing beauty of the river, applauding with childish glee the wild flowers on the banks, or the rippling reflections in the water.

'Look, look!' she cried once, pointing skyward. He stared upwards, expecting a balloon at least. But it was only 'Keats' little rosy cloud', she explained. It was not her fault if he did not find the excursion unreservedly idyllic.

'How stupid,' she reflected, 'to keep all those nice boys cooped up reading dead languages in a spot made for life and love.'

'I'm afraid they don't disturb the dead languages so much as you think,' he reassured her, smiling. 'And there will be plenty of love-making during Commem.'

'I am so glad. I suppose there are lots of engagements that week.'

'Oh, yes—but not one per cent come to anything.'

'Really? Oh, how fickle men are!'

That seemed rather question-begging, but he was so thrilled by the implicit revelation that she could not even imagine feminine inconstancy, that he forebore to draw her attention to her inadequate logic.

So childish and thoughtless indeed was she that day that nothing would content her but attending a 'Viva', which he had incautiously informed her was public.

'Nobody will notice us,' she urged with strange unconsciousness of her loveliness. 'Besides, they don't know I'm not your sister.'

'The Oxford intellect is sceptical,' he said, laughing. 'It cultivates philosophical doubt.'

But, putting a bold face on the matter, and assuming a fraternal air, he took her to the torture-chamber, in which candidates sat dolefully on a row of chairs against the wall, waiting their turn to come before the three grand inquisitors at the table. Fortunately, Winifred and he were the only spectators; but unfortunately they blundered in at the very moment when the poor owner of the punt was on the rack. The central inquisitor was trying to extract from him information about Becket, almost prompting him with the very words, but without penetrating through the duncical denseness. John Lefolle breathed more freely when the Crusades were broached; but, alas, it very soon became evident that the dunce had by no means 'got hold of the thing'. As the dunce passed out sadly, obviously ploughed, John Lefolle suffered more than he. So conscience-stricken was he that, when he had accompanied Winifred as far as her hotel, he refused her invitation to come in, pleading the compulsoriness of duty and dinner in Hall. But he could not get away without promising to call in during the evening.

The prospect of this visit was with him all through dinner, at once tempting and terrifying. Assuredly there was a skeleton at his feast, as he sat at the high table, facing the Master. The venerable portraits round the Hall seemed to rebuke his romantic waywardness. In the common-room, he sipped his port uneasily, listening as in a daze to the discussion on Free Will, which an eminent stranger had stirred up. How academic it seemed, compared with the passionate realities of life. But somehow he found himself lingering on at the academic discussion, postponing the realities of life. Every now and again, he was impelled to glance at his watch; but suddenly murmuring, 'It is very late,' he pulled himself together, and took leave of his learned brethren. But in the street the sight of a telegraph office drew his steps to it, and almost mechanically he wrote out the message: 'Regret detained. Will call early in morning.'

When he did call in the morning, he was told she had gone back to London the night before on receipt of a telegram. He turned away with a bitter pang of disappointment and regret.

IV

Their subsequent correspondence was only the more amorous. The reason she had fled from the hotel, she explained, was that she could not endure the night in those stuffy quarters. He consoled himself with the hope of seeing much of her during the Long Vacation. He did see her once at her own reception, but this time her husband wandered about the two rooms. The cosy corner was impossible, and they could only manage to gasp out a few mutual endearments amid the buzz and movement, and to arrange a *rendezvous* for the end of July. When the day came, he received a heart-broken letter, stating that her husband had borne her away to Goodwood. In a postscript she informed him that

'Quicksilver was a sure thing'. Much correspondence passed without another meeting being effected, and he lent her five pounds to pay a debt of honour incurred through her husband's 'absurd confidence in Quicksilver'. A week later this horsey husband of hers brought her on to Brighton for the races there, and hither John Lefolle flew. But her husband shadowed her, and he could only lift his hat to her as they passed each other on the Lawns. Sometimes he saw her sitting pensively on a chair while her lord and thrasher perused a pink sporting-paper. Such tantalizing proximity raised their correspondence through the Hove Post Office to fever heat. Life apart, they felt, was impossible, and, removed from the sobering influences of his cap and gown, John Lefolle dreamed of throwing everything to the winds. His literary reputation had opened out a new career. The Winifred lyrics alone had brought in a tidy sum, and though he had expended that and more on despatches of flowers and trifles to her, yet he felt this extravagance would become extinguished under daily companionship, and the poems provoked by her charms would go far towards their daily maintenance. Yes, he could throw up the University. He would rescue her from this bully, this gentleman bruiser. They would live openly and nobly in the world's eye. A poet was not even expected to be conventional.

She, on her side, was no less ardent for the great step. She raged against the world's law, the injustice by which a husband's cruelty was not sufficient ground for divorce. 'But we finer souls must take the law into our own hands,' she wrote. 'We must teach society that the ethics of a barbarous age are unfitted for our century of enlightenment.' But somehow the actual time and place of the elopement could never get itself fixed. In September her husband dragged her to Scotland, in October after the pheasants. When the dramatic day was actually fixed, Winifred wrote by the next post deferring it for a week. Even the few actual preliminary meetings they planned for Kensington Gardens or Hampstead Heath rarely came off. He lived in a whirling atmosphere of express letters of excuse, and telegrams that transformed the situation from hour to hour. Not that her passion in any way abated, or her romantic resolution really altered: it was only that her conception of time and place and ways and means was dizzily mutable.

But after nigh six months of palpitating negotiations with the adorable Mrs. Glamorys, the poet, in a moment of dejection, penned the prose apophthegm, 'It is of no use trying to change a changeable person.'

V

But at last she astonished him by a sketch plan of the elopement, so detailed, even to band-boxes and the Paris night route *via* Dieppe, that no further room for doubt was left in his intoxicated soul, and he was actually further astonished when, just as he was putting his hand-bag into the hansom, a telegram was handed to him saying: 'Gone to Homburg. Letter follows.'

He stood still for a moment on the pavement in utter distraction. What did it mean? Had she failed him again? Or was it simply that she had changed the city of refuge from Paris to Homburg? He was about to name the new station to the cabman, but then, 'letter follows'. Surely that meant that he was to wait for it. Perplexed and miserable, he stood with the telegram crumpled up in his fist. What a ridiculous situation! He had wrought himself up to the point of breaking with the world and his past, and now—it only remained to satisfy the cabman!

He tossed feverishly all night, seeking to soothe himself, but really exciting himself the more by a hundred plausible explanations. He was now strung up to such a pitch of uncertainty that he was astonished for the third time when the 'letter' did duly 'follow'.

'Dearest,' it ran, 'as I explained in my telegram, my husband became suddenly ill'—('if she *had* only put that in the telegram,' he groaned)—'and was ordered to Homburg. Of course it was impossible to leave him in this crisis, both for practical and sentimental reasons. You yourself, darling, would not like me to have aggravated his illness by my flight just at this moment, and thus possibly have his death on my conscience.' ('Darling, you are always right,' he said, kissing the letter.) 'Let us possess our souls in patience a little longer. I need not tell you how vexatious it will be to find myself nursing him in Homburg—out of the season even—instead of the prospect to which I had looked forward with my whole heart and soul. But what can one do? How true is the French proverb, 'Nothing happens but the unexpected'! Write to me immediately *Poste Restante*, that I may at least console myself with your dear words.'

The unexpected did indeed happen. Despite draughts of Elizabeth-brunnen and promenades on the Kurhaus terrace, the stalwart woman beater succumbed to his malady. The curt telegram from Winifred gave no indication of her emotions. He sent a reply-telegram of sympathy with her trouble. Although he could not pretend to grieve at this sudden providential solution of their life-problem, still he did sincerely sympathize with the distress inevitable in connection with a death, especially on foreign soil.

He was not able to see her till her husband's body had been brought across the North Sea and committed to the green repose of the old Hampstead churchyard. He found her pathetically altered—her face wan and spiritualized, and all in subtle harmony with the exquisite black gown. In the first interview, he did not dare speak of their love at all. They discussed the immortality of the soul, and she quoted George Herbert. But with the weeks the question of their future began to force its way back to his lips.

'We could not decently marry before six months,' she said, when definitely confronted with the problem.

'Six months!' he gasped.

'Well, surely you don't want to outrage everybody,' she said, pouting.

At first he was outraged himself. What! She who had been ready to flutter the world with a fantastic dance was now measuring her footsteps. But on reflection he saw that Mrs. Glamorys was right once more. Since Providence had been good enough to rescue them, why should they fly in its face? A little patience, and a blameless happiness lay before them. Let him not blind himself to the immense relief he really felt at being spared social obloquy. After all, a poet could be unconventional in his *work*—he had no need of the practical outlet demanded for the less gifted.

VI

They scarcely met at all during the next six months—it had, naturally, in this grateful reaction against their recklessness, become a sacred period, even more charged with tremulous emotion than the engagement periods of those who have not so nearly scorched themselves. Even in her presence he found a certain pleasure in combining distant adoration with the confident expectation of proximity, and thus she was restored to the sanctity which she had risked by her former easiness. And so all was for the best in the best of all possible worlds.

When the six months had gone by, he came to claim her hand. She was quite astonished. 'You promised to marry me at the end of six months,' he reminded her.

'Surely it isn't six months already,' she said.

He referred her to the calendar, recalled the date of her husband's death.

'You are strangely literal for a poet,' she said. 'Of course I *said* six months, but six months doesn't mean twenty-six weeks by the clock. All I meant was that a decent period must intervene. But even to myself it seems only yesterday that poor Harold was walking beside me in the Kurhaus Park.' She burst into tears, and in the face of them he could not pursue the argument.

Gradually, after several interviews and letters, it was agreed that they should wait another six months.

'She *is* right,' he reflected again. 'We have waited so long, we may as well wait a little longer and leave malice no handle.'

The second six months seemed to him much longer than the first. The charm of respectful adoration had lost its novelty, and once again his breast was racked by fitful fevers which could scarcely calm themselves even by conversion into sonnets. The one point of repose was that shining fixed star of marriage. Still smarting under Winifred's reproach of his unpoetic literality, he did not intend to force her to marry him exactly at the end of the twelve-month. But he was determined that she should have no later than this exact date for at least 'naming the day'. Not the most punctilious stickler for convention, he felt, could deny that Mrs. Grundy's claim had been paid to the last minute.

The publication of his new volume—containing the Winifred lyrics—had served to colour these months of intolerable delay. Even the reaction of the critics against his poetry, that conventional revolt against every second volume, that parrot cry of over-praise from the very throats that had praised him, though it pained and perplexed him, was perhaps really helpful. At any rate, the long waiting was over at last. He felt like Jacob after his years of service for Rachel.

The fateful morning dawned bright and blue, and, as the towers of Oxford were left behind him he recalled that distant Saturday when he had first gone down to meet the literary lights of London in his publisher's salon. How much older he was now than then—and yet how much younger! The nebulous melancholy of youth, the clouds of philosophy, had vanished before this beautiful creature of sunshine whose radiance cut out a clear line for his future through the confusion of life.

At a florist's in the High Street of Hampstead he bought a costly bouquet of white flowers, and walked airily to the house and rang the bell jubilantly. He could scarcely believe his ears when the maid told him her mistress was not at home. How dared the girl stare at him so impassively? Did she not know by what appointment—on what errand—he had come? Had he not written to her mistress a week ago that he would present himself that afternoon?

'Not at home!' he gasped. 'But when will she be home?'

'I fancy she won't be long. She went out an hour ago, and she has an appointment with her dressmaker at five.'

'Do you know in what direction she'd have gone?'

'Oh, she generally walks on the Heath before tea.'

The world suddenly grew rosy again. 'I will come back again,' he said. Yes, a walk in this glorious air—heathward—would do him good.

As the door shut he remembered he might have left the flowers, but he would not ring again, and besides, it was, perhaps, better he should present them with his own hand, than let her find them on the hall table. Still, it seemed rather awkward to walk about the streets with a bouquet, and he was glad, accidentally to strike the old Hampstead Church, and to seek a momentary seclusion in passing through its avenue of quiet gravestones on his heathward way.

Mounting the few steps, he paused idly a moment on the verge of this green 'God's-acre' to read a perpendicular slab on a wall, and his face broadened into a smile as he followed the absurdly elaborate biography of a rich, self-made merchant who had taught himself to read, 'Reader, go thou and do likewise,' was the delicious bull at the end. As he turned away, the smile still lingering about his lips, he saw a dainty figure tripping down the stony graveyard path, and though he was somehow startled to find her still in black, there was no mistaking Mrs. Glamorys. She ran to meet him with a glad cry, which filled his eyes with happy tears.

'How good of you to remember!' she said, as she took the bouquet from his unresisting hand, and turned again on her footsteps. He followed her wonderingly across the uneven road towards a narrow aisle of graves on the left. In another instant she has stooped before a shining white stone, and laid his bouquet reverently upon it. As he reached her side, he saw that his flowers were almost lost in the vast mass of floral offerings with which the grave of the woman beater was bestrewn.

'How good of you to remember the anniversary,' she murmured again.

'How could I forget it?' he stammered, astonished. 'Is not this the end of the terrible twelve-month?'

The soft gratitude died out of her face. 'Oh, is *that* what you were thinking of?'

'What else?' he murmured, pale with conflicting emotions.

'What else! I think decency demanded that this day, at least, should be sacred to his memory. Oh, what brutes men are!' And she burst into tears.

     Victorian Short Stories: Stories of Courtship

His patient breast revolted at last. 'You said *he* was the brute!' he retorted, outraged.

'Is that your chivalry to the dead? Oh, my poor Harold, my poor Harold!'

For once her tears could not extinguish the flame of his anger. 'But you told me he beat you,' he cried.

'And if he did, I dare say I deserved it. Oh, my darling, my darling!' She laid her face on the stone and sobbed.

John Lefolle stood by in silent torture. As he helplessly watched her white throat swell and fall with the sobs, he was suddenly struck by the absence of the black velvet band—the truer mourning she had worn in the lifetime of the so lamented. A faint scar, only perceptible to his conscious eye, added to his painful bewilderment.

At last she rose and walked unsteadily forward. He followed her in mute misery. In a moment or two they found themselves on the outskirts of the deserted heath. How beautiful stretched the gorsy rolling country! The sun was setting in great burning furrows of gold and green—a panorama to take one's breath away. The beauty and peace of Nature passed into the poet's soul.

'Forgive me, dearest,' he begged, taking her hand.

She drew it away sharply. 'I cannot forgive you. You have shown yourself in your true colours.'

Her unreasonableness angered him again. 'What do you mean? I only came in accordance with our long-standing arrangement. You have put me off long enough.'

'It is fortunate I did put you off long enough to discover what you are.'

He gasped. He thought of all the weary months of waiting, all the long comedy of telegrams and express letters, the far-off flirtations of the cosy corner, the baffled elopement to Paris. 'Then you won't marry me?'

'I cannot marry a man I neither love nor respect.'

'You don't love me!' Her spontaneous kiss in his sober Oxford study seemed to burn on his angry lips.

'No, I never loved you.'

He took her by the arms and turned her round roughly. 'Look me in the face and dare to say you have never loved me.'

His memory was buzzing with passionate phrases from her endless letters. They stung like a swarm of bees. The sunset was like blood-red mist before his eyes.

'I have never loved you,' she said obstinately.

'You——!' His grasp on her arms tightened. He shook her.

'You are bruising me,' she cried.

His grasp fell from her arms as though they were red-hot. He had become a woman beater.

www.ingramcontent.com/pod-product-compliance
Lightning Source LLC
LaVergne TN
LVHW041726190726
843493LV00007B/2222